CANDLELIGHT REGENCIES

- 257 THE CHEVALIER'S LADY, *Betty Hale Hyatt*
- 263 MOONLIGHT MIST, *Laura London*
- 501 THE SCANDALOUS SEASON, *Nina Pykare*
- 505 THE BARTERED BRIDE, *Anne Hillary*
- 512 BRIDE OF TORQUAY, *Lucy Phillips Stewart*
- 515 MANNER OF A LADY, *Cilla Whitmore*
- 521 LOVE'S CAPTIVE, *Samantha Lester*
- 527 KITTY, *Jennie Tremaine*
- 530 BRIDE OF A STRANGER, *Lucy Phillips Stewart*
- 537 HIS LORDSHIP'S LANDLADY, *Cilla Whitmore*
- 542 DAISY, *Jennie Tremaine*
- 543 THE SLEEPING HEIRESS, *Phyllis Taylor Pianka*
- 548 LOVE IN DISGUISE, *Nina Pykare*
- 549 THE RUNAWAY HEIRESS, *Lillian Cheatham*
- 554 A MAN OF HER CHOOSING, *Nina Pykare*
- 555 PASSING FANCY, *Mary Linn Roby*
- 562 LUCY, *Jennie Tremaine*
- 563 PIPPA, *Megan O'Connor*
- 570 THOMASINA, *Joan Vincent*
- 571 SENSIBLE CECILY, *Margaret Summerville*
- 572 DOUBLE FOLLY, *Marnie Ellingson*
- 573 POLLY, *Jennie Tremaine*
- 578 THE MISMATCHED LOVERS, *Anne Hillary*
- 579 UNWILLING BRIDE, *Marnie Ellingson*
- 580 INFAMOUS ISABELLE, *Margaret Summerville*
- 581 THE DAZZLED HEART, *Nina Pykare*
- 586 THE EDUCATION OF JOANNE, *Joan Vincent*
- 587 MOLLY, *Jennie Tremaine*
- 588 JESSICA WINDOM, *Marnie Ellingson*
- 589 THE ARDENT SUITOR, *Marian Lorraine*
- 593 THE RAKE'S COMPANION, *Regina Towers*
- 594 LADY INCOGNITA, *Nina Pykare*
- 595 A BOND OF HONOUR, *Joan Vincent*
- 596 GINNY, *Jennie Tremaine*
- 597 THE MARRIAGE AGREEMENT, *Margaret MacWilliams*
- 602 A COMPANION IN JOY, *Dorothy Mack*
- 603 MIDNIGHT SURRENDER, *Margaret Major Cleaves*
- 604 A SCHEME FOR LOVE, *Joan Vincent*
- 605 THE DANGER IN LOVING, *Helen Nuelle*
- 610 LOVE'S FOLLY, *Nina Pykare*
- 611 A WORTHY CHARADE, *Vivian Harris*
- 612 THE DUKE'S WARD, *Samantha Lester*
- 613 MANSION FOR A LADY, *Cilla Whitmore*

SARATOGA SEASON

Margaret MacWilliams

A CANDLELIGHT EDWARDIAN SPECIAL

Published by
Dell Publishing Co., Inc.
1 Dag Hammarskjold Plaza
New York, New York 10017

Copyright © 1980 by Margaret MacWilliams

All rights reserved. No part of this book may be
reproduced or tranmitted in any form or by any
means, electronic or mechanical, including photocopying,
recording, or by any information storage and retrieval
system, without the written permission of the Publisher,
except where permitted by law.

Dell ® TM 681510, Dell Publishing Co., Inc.

ISBN: 0-440-18081-3

Printed in the United States of America
First printing—November 1980

To Abigail Mae MacWilliams

SARATOGA
SEASON

Chapter One

"What are we going to do about Abigail?" Mrs. Chauncey Worth asked her husband, a plaintive, querulous note creeping into her voice, which invariably occurred whenever she broached the subject of her stepdaughter.

They were seated in the breakfast room of their Victorian mansion in Saratoga, the warm August sunlight streaming through the plate-glass windows, setting the silver service aglow and highlighting the intricate pile of golden curls amassed on the top of Mrs. Chauncey Worth's imperious head.

When her husband did not reply, she straightened the bodice of her white lace peignoir with an impatient jerk and allowed a slight frown to mar the alabaster smoothness of her forehead. *Really*, she sputtered inwardly, *Chauncey can be such a bore and I would have certainly thought twice about marrying him if I had suspected that all he would ever think of was his horses.* Her large China-blue eyes, usually placid and expressionless, fastened on her husband with a look bordering on distaste.

Absentmindedly Chauncey Worth stirred his cup of coffee, heavily laced with cream, let out a satisfied grunt, and with an air of triumph glanced up from the morning newspaper.

"My dear Clarissa," he exclaimed, "Did you know that Sabrina pulled a leg muscle at Pimlico? That opens up all sorts of possibilities for My Clarissa. I must get right over to the track to catch her morning workout."

Clarissa Worth bit her lower lip and with difficulty restrained from informing her husband that she had never been overly pleased having a horse named after her. In the dark hours of the night when sleep escaped her as Chauncey snored contentedly by her side, she was quite certain that if her husband had to choose between shedding his horses or his wife, the former would win hands down.

"What's wrong with Abigail?" Chauncey asked, revealing to his wife's surprise that he had actually heard her question. "She is a healthy eighteen-year-old who is happier riding horseback than being on the dance floor. Now, tell me, what's wrong with that?"

Clarissa Worth sighed. "There is nothing wrong with being healthy and enjoying riding," she answered, struggling to sound patient. "But

Chauncey, darling, surely you must realize that Abigail lacks all of the social graces, and what is even more disturbing, she is not the least interested in acquiring them.

"Do you want your daughter to end up an old maid, or worse yet marry one of the stable boys? I've tried, Chauncey, believe me I've tried, but it isn't easy when one marries to inherit a stepdaughter not many years younger than oneself. And I must admit to utter and abysmal defeat as far as Abigail is concerned."

"I think you've managed very well," he protested mildly. "Her debutante ball last winter was a great success and she never seemed to lack for escorts to all the other festivities. Why, you were saying only yesterday that Freddie Freyhuysing is completely overboard about her."

"But don't you see?" Clarissa Worth replied, wondering why men in general and Chauncey in particular were so obtuse where affairs of the heart were concerned. "She merely tolerates him, and it's not just Freddie she treats that way, for there are quite a few others I could mention. If she keeps on rejecting suitors, in a few months there won't be a beau in sight. Chauncey, do you realize this winter she will be a *post*-debutante?" And the way she emphasized the word "post" made it seem that such a predicament would be a major catastrophe comparable to sudden death or a terminal illness.

Chauncey Worth had finished his coffee, and like a racehorse at the starting line who prances about eager to hear the opening gun, he was halfway out the door of the breakfast room when he sensed it would be wise to take the time to appease his wife of a little less than a year, whose tiresome tantrums and complaints had unfortunately not surfaced until after the wedding.

"Abby's all right," he called over his shoulder in a reassuring tone. "So don't you worry your pretty little head about her. She reminds me of her mother, who, I'm sure you've been told, developed into a great beauty."

"Yes, I've been told that far too frequently," Mrs. Worth muttered as she watched her husband's rotund figure disappear from view.

Pouring herself a second cup of coffee, Clarissa Worth began to peruse the pile of creamy-white invitations lying on the breakfast table. Being the wife of Chauncey Worth did have its compensations, she conceded, for it meant being a member of the charmed inner circle of Saratoga society, asked automatically to all of the balls and festivities that were jammed into a very brief but exciting Season.

Frowning as she arose from the breakfast table to retire to the writing room, she recalled Chauncey's last remark about the beauty of his first wife and her narrow lips tightened into a thin, hard line as she decided that the portrait of the first Mrs. Chauncey Worth, which dominated the drawing room of the Fifth Avenue town house, would be removed, if not immediately upon their return to New York in September, then shortly thereafter.

Abigail Worth, blissfully unaware that she was a topic of discussion at the family breakfast table, was riding her favorite mare, Matilda, along a wooded trail that abutted her father's property. She had struggled out of bed long before the lowliest servant in the household had arisen to stoke the kitchen fires, and being quite certain that most of Saratoga still slept, had not bothered to dress in her formal riding habit. Instead she had put on a pair of corduroy knickers filched from her father's dressing room.

As Chauncey Worth's waistline had long since succumbed to such delightful temptations as french pastries, triple-layer cakes, and a goodly number of after-dinner brandies, Abigail, as slender as a young birch tree, found it necessary to tie a rope around her waist. A white shirt open at the throat completed the outfit, which, according to Saratoga standards, would have been considered—at the very least—bizarre.

She whistled softly as she crossed the wide green lawns still wet with dew, savoring the marvelous sensation that while Saratoga slept, she was awake, experiencing the beauty of a spectacular sunrise as she breathed in deeply the sweet scent of the pines. For a brief time she knew she would be in control of her destiny.

Reaching the stable, she selected a Western saddle in place of the smart English sidesaddle her father had had especially made for her at Martin and Martin of Philadelphia. Matilda, hearing her approach, was already stamping and neighing in her stall.

"Be quiet, Matilda," she whispered urgently, and at the sound of Abigail's voice Matilda flashed her mistress a conspiratorial look and meekly allowed herself to be prepared for their journey.

Emerging from the stables, Abigail held the mare to a walk until, gaining the protection of the woods with its maze of bridle paths, she urged Matilda into a canter. She had allotted herself one hour for this particular adventure, knowing that by then the servants would be stirring and it would be quite a trick to return Matilda to her stall and slip into the house undetected. But the risk involved only served to add an extra fillip of spice to her escapade.

Archibald Pomeroy III sat on the bank of the Kayaderosseras Creek, savoring the stillness around him, broken only by the pleasant gurgling of the stream as it raced over the stones and rocks that had, over the years, grown smooth from the constant flow of water.

Wearing disreputable overalls that should long since have been patched or preferably discarded, he concluded that last night he and his mother had reached a very amicable compromise.

When the chips were down, he thought, she was really a most understanding woman, and although he knew she had been looking forward to watching her only son become immersed in the endless round of social events of the Saratoga Season, she had succeeded in hiding her disappointment, not even mentioning that the invitations to a ball she had been planning in his honor had already been addressed and were lying neatly stacked on her writing desk, ready to be mailed.

Sitting with his back propped against a huge boulder, chewing on a pencil, and frowning at the blank pages of his notebook, Archibald ran a hand through his wiry red hair. Last night he had promised to stay with his mother at their home, The Elms, for the duration of the month of August, and she in turn had promised that his presence would remain a closely guarded secret, giving him the opportunity to concentrate on his novel.

"I'm tired of hops and balls," he had confided to her. "And the races have never entranced me. In addition, I'm terribly bored with debutantes and post-debutantes whose mothers have channeled their energies into a single direction—to find an acceptable husband for their daughters. Sometimes I heartily wish I had two heads—that would scratch me, once and for all, from the list of eligible bachelors."

He hesitated a moment before plunging onward to make a confession he should have made some time ago. "Besides, I must tell you I have proposed to Lady Ursula Huntington and she has accepted me, so that puts me completely out of the running."

Mrs. Pomeroy studied him with troubled eyes. "Archie, dear, do you really love her?" she asked, silently doubting if anyone could love Lady Ursula—a formidable, statuesque English woman with faded yellow hair and a nose some called aristocratic but Mrs. Pomeroy considered far too long. In addition, when she smiled, which was most infrequently, it seemed to be a very painful experience, leading Archibald's mother to suspect that ice water flowed in her veins.

"Love!" Archibald replied scornfully. "What has love got to do with it? Intellectually we are completely in tune, and that's the vital ingredient, Mother."

Edwina Pomeroy sighed, abandoning the temptation to pursue the matter one step further, for she had recently learned, to her sorrow, that there was nobody anywhere in the world more opinionated than a young man who had graduated from Harvard with honors before spending two years at Oxford, and was at the present time engaged in writing his first novel, which he fully expected would electrify the literary world.

Realizing that any advice she might give him would simply be brushed aside, she concluded that she could only hope her son would see Lady Ursula as others saw her before he took those fatal steps to the altar.

So Mrs. Pomeroy merely sighed and continued to gaze fondly at her handsome son. She was a tall striking woman, an aristocrat to her fingertips, with snow-white hair that added rather than detracted from her appearance, her doelike brown eyes reflecting compassion and understanding. Heaven knows, she admitted, she had responded often enough in the same way to the Saratoga Season, thankful that when she chose she could cloister herself in their estate on the outskirts of the village, away from the hotel piazzas and the daily monotony of the morning trip to the springs, followed by the afternoon parade of carriages along Broadway. Therefore, how could she possibly fault her son for reacting the same way?

"I understand, dear, your desire to avoid the Season," she said lightly, and then she laughed a warm, perceptive laugh. "You know, I've always suspected your father, at your age, felt exactly the same way, for remember I was once a debutante on the prowl. You'd think by eighteen ninety-four women in the upper classes would be allowed to contemplate other careers but marriage, but unfortunately times haven't changed very much since I was a girl."

She sighed and then suddenly changed the subject. "Now, tell me what you intend to do. Return to London? I imagine your father is rather lonely rattling about in the Embassy."

He shook his head. "No, I want to stay right here. It's a chance for you and me to see something of each other and it will give me time to work on my novel. Couldn't I be sort of incognito?"

She looked at him doubtfully, amused that her son had no conception of the stir his presence would create among the social set and that it would take only one brief excursion into Saratoga for the word to spread like wildfire that he had returned from England.

"No," she said firmly. "That wouldn't be practical. You'll simply have to stay here in hiding. We'll caution the servants, of course, and I'm certain they can be trusted."

"Let's try it," he urged, and so they had reached an agreement, solemnly finalizing it over a glass of sherry.

This morning he had arisen early before dawn and, saddling his horse, had ridden to this isolated spot, determined to discipline himself and begin Chapter One without delay. But he had no sooner started the first sentence, when he heard footsteps on the path to the creek and a young girl emerged from behind the thicket. Startled, he dropped his pencil and then found himself wordlessly gaping at the strangest apparition he had ever seen in Saratoga, Boston, New York, or London.

"Where in the world did you come from?" he finally managed to ask, his eyes at first fastened on her peculiar outfit before traveling to her thick black hair, which was in complete disarray.

"I don't believe I should tell you," she replied with spirit, "for it might land me in all sorts of trouble."

His first annoyance at being disturbed was rapidly replaced by amusement and curiosity and she saw that his hazel eyes were dancing. "Let's see if I can guess," he said. "You're not a spy, by chance, working for some foreign government?"

Her cobalt-blue eyes were dancing too as, joining in the game, she shook her head slowly and said, "No—try again."

"Could you be a lady's maid engaged in a lark while your mistress is still asleep, dreaming of last night's flirtations?"

Abigail hesitated before deciding that the second explanation was relatively plausible. "How clever you are to have guessed," she cried out. "You happen to be absolutely right. I'm employed by a very tiresome person, the second wife of

Mr. Chauncey Worth. Do you happen to know her?"

"Do you do this sort of thing frequently?" he asked, bypassing her question.

"I do—despite the great risk involved—for if I'm ever found out, I'll surely be sacked."

"This Mrs. Worth," he asked. "Why do you consider her so tiresome?"

Abigail frowned and settled herself on a nearby boulder. Suddenly aware that her hair was windblown, she smoothed it back from her face before replying. "Because she represents everything I abhor. She is flighty, silly, and worst of all not too bright. All she thinks about are parties and balls and what gowns to wear. Don't you think the idle rich are complete and utter frauds?"

"Well, not all of them." He tossed her a quizzical look. "Tell me," he asked, "are you in the habit of making such sweeping statements? For I must confess some of the rich appear quite tolerable to me."

"Name one," she said with an air of defiance.

"Let me see . . . the Pomeroys for example. Their property lies over there." He gestured across the creek to the fields and meadows that lay beyond the woods.

She was studying him with interest, noting the disreputable overalls, the tattered shirt, and that in addition he was barefoot.

"How come you know the Pomeroys?" she flung

back. "Are you their butler or perhaps their footman?" Her voice revealed that she considered his holding either position extremely unlikely.

Archibald paused, searching for the proper cover, angry at himself for introducing his family name into the conversation. At last he hit upon what he considered a credible solution. "No, I'm a farmer, their tenant farmer actually. I work the acreage around the estate. Of course, the family is there only during August, now that Mr. Pomeroy is ambassador to England. Although I see very little of them, I consider them decent people."

Abigail was chewing thoughtfully on a blade of grass. "If you're a farmer," she challenged, "why aren't you on the farm now, milking the cows?"

"My dear young lady," he answered, giving her a patronizing look. "You certainly know next to nothing about farming and as I never neglect my duties, let me inform you that the cows were milked by me long before sunrise and at the present moment are grazing contentedly in their pasture. Besides, a farmer is entitled to some time off, don't you think?"

"But of course. Tell me, where do you usually spend your free time?"

"Often right here. It's one of my favorite spots."

"Mine too—funny we haven't met before."

"You have another question?"

"How did you guess?"

"By the expression on your face. It lights up

like a Christmas tree and I can see the question forming before you ask it."

"You are clairvoyant."

"I hope so, for you see I don't intend to be a farmer all my life. I want to write."

"That was going to be my next question. I saw the pad and pencil. Tell me what are you writing? I find this all most exciting."

"I'm writing about Saratoga in August," he replied. Having told one white lie, he saw no reason for not telling another. Besides, he doubted if this chit of a girl would have the slightest interest in the social history of England, which was his rather heavy subject.

"I can't imagine anyone wanting to write about that," she said emphatically. "It's always the same year after year."

"But that's where you're wrong," he protested. "There's a vast audience out there fascinated by the shenanigans of the very rich. That was why I was so intrigued when you told me you worked for the Chauncey Worths. Don't you see what a marvelous coincidence this has become? I'm on the outside looking in, while you're on the inside looking out, in a perfect position to give me all sorts of engaging tidbits of information. A writer must be able to inject realism into his stories, and you will be able to provide me with what I desperately need."

"I do hear lots of gossip," she admitted with

some reluctance, feeling a slight twinge of guilt at the prospect of letting her own class down.

"I'm sure you do. Will you pass it on to me?"

She hesitated briefly and then, throwing her cap to the winds, capitulated with a vigorous yes. To her surprise she was finding this farm boy an engaging companion and a little warning bell inside her head rang, telling her to be wary that this strikingly handsome man did not become too irresistible.

"Splendid! But tell me a little more about your duties. Are they very onerous?" he asked. "It might help me in my research."

As she sat there on the boulder he studied the slender outline of her body with more than casual interest and wondered if she had the slightest notion of what a charming picture she presented. She was like an unruly colt who had yet to be tamed and groomed, and he felt an unexpected tug of regret that far too soon she would be fashioned into a mold, a stylized mold, and without realizing it she would become just another young lady among so many presented to society; one in a stable of hopefuls on parade with a prestigious marriage in view. For, of course, there was no doubt in his mind she was no more a lady's maid than he was a farmer.

"It's all very tedious," she said with a deep sigh. "I am constantly at her beck and call, assisting her with this and that, helping her to decide what gown to wear to a particular function. I'm expert at arranging her hair and when she leaves for a glamorous evening, perfectly attired, I return to my narrow and extremely uncomfortable cot in the attic and wonder why fate made me a lady's maid."

"It must be a very difficult assignment," he said consolingly.

"Very difficult, yes—but so far I have managed to survive."

"It certainly must take a lot of courage to sneak out of the house and go riding."

"Tommy, one of the grooms, would do anything for me," she confided. "He looks the other way when I return Matilda. And the kitchen help are also on my side. It's sort of a conspiracy to see how much we can get away with.

"At least it relieves the monotony of the days. I'm more fortunate as I spend most of my time in the out-of-doors. I should hate to be housebound."

He glanced at his watch and pulled himself hastily to his feet. "It's getting late. I must return to feed the chickens. Shouldn't you be going too?"

She clapped her hands over her mouth stifling a horrified gasp, and without as much as a goodbye she darted down the narrow path to where she had tethered her horse.

But he was close behind her, and as she vaulted into the saddle he grabbed Matilda's reins. "Tomorrow—same time, same place?" he asked.

"Yes, yes," she cried out hurriedly. "Now let me go, please."

"By the way, what's your name?" he demanded, still refusing to release his grip.

"Annie." She tossed the name to him over her shoulder, and grabbing the reins with a quick wave of her hand, galloped down the bridle path and out of sight.

After she had departed he settled down once more to write but soon discarded any attempt to do so, discovering that the tantalizing vision of a mischievous girl stealing from the house for an early morning canter was disturbing his serious train of thought.

She can't be much over sixteen, he guessed, and from the lofty age of twenty-five that seemed extremely young indeed. Still reluctant to return to his work, he began to wonder what she would look like in formal riding clothes or on her way to a fancy dress ball, and it never occurred to him that it might be considered strange that a man recently betrothed to one girl could find another so intriguing.

Chapter Two

As Abigail approached the stables in the rear of the house, she saw that she was indeed late. Lights shone in the kitchen, the breakfast room, and her father's and stepmother's suite on the second floor.

"Bother," she muttered. Reaching the stables, she tossed Matilda's reins to the groom. "Rub her down well, Tommy, please," she said quickly, and she knew it was not necessary to say another word, for Tommy and she had long since become friends and not only was his loyalty without question, but her frequent unconventional activities added a considerable enjoyment to his otherwise mundane existence.

Entering the kitchen wing, she had one foot on the first step of the back stairway when Daniel, her four-year-old spaniel, who was warming his rump by the kitchen stove, spotted her and, letting out a yelp of pleasure, bounded in her direction.

Olivia, the colored cook, dropped a spoon on the stove with a clatter and approached, arms akimbo, with an angry glint in her eyes.

"And what have you been up to this time, Miss Abigail?" she demanded. A tiny wisp of a woman of indeterminate age, she barred Abigail's attempt to escape up the stairs.

"Nothing much," Abigail replied. "Merely an early morning canter. Certainly there's nothing wrong in that."

"In those clothes! I do declare if Mrs. Worth knew about this, she'd tell you off in no uncertain terms."

"But she won't know," Abigail replied serenely. "Unless, of course, you should tell her, Olivia."

The cook's wrinkled face, which resembled the intricate network of byways that crisscrossed the country, broke into a sympathetic grin. "No, I won't tell, and that's half the problem around here because you know I never will. But I'm warning you right here and now, Miss Abigail, unless you mend your ways, you're headed for trouble, big trouble."

"I promise I'll be a perfect lady the rest of the day," Abigail declared and with a breezy wave of her hand she scurried up the stairs, looking forward to the luxury of a leisurely hot bath.

Humming to herself, she turned on the faucets in the high metal tub in her bathroom and gave herself up to the exquisite delight of reliving the unexpected and exciting early morning meeting by the Kayaderosseras Creek.

A farmer, she thought, and giggled as she imagined her stepmother's reaction if she should have the slightest inkling of what had occurred.

But an extremely refined farmer, Abigail concluded as she climbed into the tub and searched for the soap, for it had not escaped her notice that his fingers were well manicured and she had always imagined that farmers' hands would be rather rough and red.

Still his clothes had certainly not been those of a gentleman and she chuckled as she pictured Freddie Freyhuysing, the epitome of the latest fashion plate, running around in bare feet.

So if he weren't the Pomeroy's tenant farmer, who was he? she mused. Unable to come up with a logical answer, she shrugged her shoulders, thinking how grossly unfair it was that someone who was probably socially unacceptable could be so terribly attractive, putting to shame the parade of possible suitors her stepmother was in the process of mobilizing for her for the month of August, with, unfortunately, Freddie Freyhuysing heading the list. Poor Freddie—an emaciated youth with prominent blue eyes who followed her around with such dogged devotion, she was frequently tempted to pat his head and give him a biscuit. And to make matters even worse, he had inherited from his father's side of the family a weak, wobbly chin—such a contrast from her recent companion, with his strong chiseled features. She sighed as she recalled how handsome and debonair he had been, stretched out on the grassy bank beside the gurgling stream.

As she climbed out of the tub, wrapping herself in a huge fleecy towel, she realized that he had never told her his name. *Annie—he thinks mine is Annie.* Chuckling, she selected a white muslin frock from her wardrobe and, slipping into it, fastened a light-blue sash around her slender waist. With a matching ribbon to hold back her heavy black hair and slippers in the same hue, she decided that she would even pass her stepmother's careful scrutiny and descended the stairs to confront her.

To Abigail the writing and breakfast rooms were the only comfortable areas in the vast Victorian-style mansion her father had built in Saratoga some years ago. Elsewhere the furniture was black walnut with complicated underpinnings, the tables marble-topped, the parquet floors hidden by ornate Aubusson rugs, and the sunlight discouraged entry because of the heavy velvet draperies drawn across the windows.

In contrast, the writing room was light and airy, with white dimity curtains and French Provincial furniture. Her father had told her once that her mother had been allowed to have free rein with its decor, and Abigail, who had only the vaguest recollection of her mother, suspected it reflected her personality. The fireplace and moldings were painted white, and over the mantel hung a Renoir, its brilliant splashes of color breathtakingly beautiful. It had been acquired by her mother on her last trip to Paris, shortly before her death, and although Chauncey Worth was more at home with the somber oil paintings of his ancestors hanging in the other rooms, he had allowed it to remain where her mother had placed it.

She found Clarissa Worth ensconced behind her writing desk. "You slept late," Clarissa remarked sharply, glancing up at the ormolu clock on the mantel. "I ordered the carriage some time ago. It should be waiting." She had changed into a pink voile dress, the skirt a mass of ruffles, and as she arose from her chair she picked up a white parasol that was liberally sprinkled with variegated shades of rosebuds.

Finding her stepdaughter for once properly attired, she gave a sigh of relief and walked from the writing room to the hallway with Abigail trailing obediently behind her. Seth, the colored butler, immaculate in his summer whites, opened the heavy door with a flourish and they proceeded together down the gravel path toward the wrought-iron fence and gate that divided their property from the broad tree-lined street.

Abigail saw to her delight that her stepmother

had ordered the surrey, which meant that she would be allowed to drive. Although it was painted a somber black, a bright-yellow fringe around the top gave it a saucy look. Tommy was holding the chestnut bay, and another groom stood to one side to assist them up the narrow steps.

People in neighboring houses were already departing for their daily pilgrimages to the springs, and by the time they reached Broadway there were carriages of every description in front of and behind them. The piazza of the United States Hotel was crowded and the sidewalks were crowded too by visitors who preferred to walk instead of ride.

Clarissa bowed to the left and to the right as they drove along, delighted that she had acquired so many friends and acquaintances in such a short span of time. Before she had had the good fortune to catch Chauncey Worth's eye at a ball in New York, she had been an aging post-debutante with the prospect of making a suitable alliance rapidly diminishing.

As he was many rungs above her on the social ladder, she as well as everyone else had been surprised when he began to court her assiduously. Recognizing that he was a very lonely man at that dangerous stage in life when the desire for a final fling takes precedence over caution, she had played her cards cleverly and won.

But since then she had learned the bitter lesson

that although her marriage to Chauncey Worth had guaranteed her an impregnable social position, it was a marriage without love and a sparsity of passion. At first he had treated her as a child to be amused and pampered, but soon tiring of the game, he had returned to his clubs and the racetracks, leaving her alone more and more frequently, feeling frustrated and neglected.

As they moved at a slow pace along Broadway, she glanced at Abigail Worth with envy and impatience—envy because the girl was young and lovely and wealthy, and with impatience because she did not seem to have the slightest inclination to capitalize on her assets.

At the Congress Spring they descended from the surrey, Abigail turning the care of it over to one of the many colored boys who hung outside the enclosure hoping to earn a penny or two.

With great dignity Clarissa opened her parasol, and holding their silver cups in their hands, they advanced toward the spring and the dipper boys, who with tin cups attached to long sticks were serving the mineral water. Their cups filled, they strolled along a path bordered on either side by neat beds of geraniums, petunias, and impatiens. The band was playing a rousing Sousa march and Abigail was forced to admit that although it was stultifying to be expected to take part in this procession every day, it was without question a gay and colorful scene.

They found seats in the pavilion, which was decorated with a profusion of hanging baskets suspended from the beamed ceiling, while the rays from the sun streaming through its stained-glass windows fashioned multicolored patterns on the tile floor and intricately scrolled woodwork.

Usually bored by the chitchat her stepmother's friends engaged in while sipping the mineral waters, today Abigail pricked up her ears and listened, hopeful to garner some spicy pieces of gossip to pass along to her new acquaintance.

The talk this morning centered around one of the grande dames of Saratoga, Mrs. Horace Vandermark, who for many years had occupied the apex of its social structure. A thoroughly disagreeable individual, feared and hated by everyone, she was nevertheless invariably treated with awe and respect, for it was well known that it was within her power to destroy a carefully preserved reputation in a matter of seconds. So when Mrs. Vandermark, seated in her favorite chair on the piazza of the United States Hotel or in the lovely elm-shaded interior garden, saw fit to scowl—which she frequently did—the coterie that always surrounded her did too.

Today in the pavilion an element of underlying excitement prevailed, for it appeared that at long last Mrs. Vandermark's timid son, who his overly possessive mother had successfully thwarted whenever he contemplated marriage, was on the verge of succumbing to wedded bliss, defying his mother's stridently voiced objections.

Every aspect of the romance was discussed, analyzed, and dissected and although it was never overtly stated, it was obvious to the most undiscerning participant that Mrs. Vandermark's friends and would-be friends were ecstatic to see the old lady in danger of going down to defeat.

Smiling, Abigail filed away all the fascinating details for future reference, and while the ladies surrounding her stepmother, having finally exhausted the main event of the season, turned to another topic, she quietly emptied her silver cup of mineral water onto a potted plant.

Soon the slow procession back to their homes and hotels began, and those who were not attending the races that day prepared for luncheon, which was to be followed by the promenade of the carriages along Broadway to the lake.

At the lunch table Clarissa remarked that she intended to take a nap and had ordered the victoria for two o'clock. "After our ride," she informed her stepdaughter, "we've been invited for tea."

Abigail's heart plummeted, for she had been about to endeavor to persuade her stepmother to allow her to be free for the balance of the afternoon, but if they had been invited to tea, she knew her request would be promptly denied.

"Where?" she asked, her usual high spirits badly deflated.

"At the Elms, with Mrs. Pomeroy." By the glow of pleasure on Clarissa's face, Abigail realized that her stepmother considered the invitation an especially important plum.

"As I'm sure you are aware," Clarissa Worth continued, "she is the wife of our present ambassador to Great Britain. In addition, her son, Archibald Pomeroy the Third, is considered the great catch of the Season. He has been in England the past few years, but now that he has returned there's no doubt but he will be relentlessly pursued. When we meet him this afternoon, as I'm hopeful we will, I trust you'll make an effort to be particularly charming. As I was saying to your father only this morning, no girl can afford to be as indifferent and casual as you, and someday I'm certain you'll regret it."

"Anyone," sniffed Abigail, "with the name of Archibald Pomeroy the Third, has got to be a prig. And the mere fact that you are plotting to ensnare him as an escort for me because he is rated 'the great catch of the Season,' I find simply nauseating."

Clarissa Worth, her China-blue eyes cold and expressionless, stared at her stepdaughter for several moments, delicately shrugging her shoulders and pulling back her chair, before she wordlessly made her departure.

Left alone in the tremendous dining room, which was frequently occupied by thirty guests,

Abigail began to have second thoughts about this afternoon's excursion. It would be a nuisance, of course, to have to change to another outfit and join the leisurely procession that wound its way to Saratoga Lake. But the prospect of tea at The Elms might be worthwhile if it gave her an opportunity to make a few subtle inquiries about the Pomeroy's farmhand.

Also, now that she had learned the Pomeroys had a son, she began to wonder if he could be the young man she had met on her early morning ride. If that proved to be the case, she decided August at Saratoga might develop into an exciting experience instead of the drab affair she had expected it to be.

What fun if they met at the tea table with no one there having the slightest notion that this was not their first encounter! With the prospect of continuing the mild deception appealing strongly to the venturesome side of Abigail's nature, she envisioned them bowing formally to each other when they were introduced, and as they chatted about such inconsequential things as the weather or the ball on Friday night, their eyes would meet and they would smile and silently agree that nothing could prevent another delightful meeting at Kayaderosseras Creek the following morning.

Chapter Three

For the promenade of the carriages Clarissa Worth had selected the family victoria. With four matched grays pulling the heavy vehicle, the silver monogrammed harnesses flashing in the sunlight and two servants in livery on the box, they presented to the gaping bystanders along the route exactly what she intended to present—great wealth and an impregnable position in society.

Relaxing against the richly upholstered black velvet seat of the carriage, holding a lace parasol in one hand, Clarissa noted with approval that today the coachman had skillfully maneuvered them until they were first in the long line of vehicles. It was a position of honor and prestige, and she smiled contentedly as they proceeded along the dirt road shaded on either side by stately elms.

Abigail was smiling too, for her stepmother's regal manner reminded her of Madame Jumel, who, back in earlier days, had been very much disliked in Saratoga, yet always managed to sweep ahead in her carriage and lead the procession.

One afternoon, looking back to enjoy the sight of a line of vehicles trailing behind her, Madame Jumel saw to her dismay that there was only one coach in the rear. It was painted yellow to match her golden equipage and drawn by four emaciated horses.

One village prankster was dressed as a coachman, and another in footman's uniform sat on top of a clothes basket, while inside a former slave was ensconced, wearing an elaborate gown, fanning himself and nodding disdainfully to the spectators, who were by this time doubled up with laughter.

Although tempted to tell her stepmother the story, Abigail refrained from doing so, suspecting she would consider it far from humorous.

As their carriage rolled along, Clarissa Worth was thinking that all in all it had been a moderately successful day. Except for that one outburst at the luncheon table, Abigail had been surprisingly demure and malleable.

Turning her head, she studied her stepdaughter and found nothing to criticize in her appearance. The sheer blue crepe-de-chine gown she was wearing was most becoming, and it was obvious she had taken a good deal of care with her appearance, for her normally unruly hair had been brushed until it shone and was arranged in soft curls about her face.

"My dear," she said almost affectionately, "I'm sure you'll find the Pomeroys charming."

When the girl did not reply, she half closed her eyes and began to picture a ball at the Grand Union with Abigail circling the room in Archibald Pomeroy's arms. It would be a splendid match that might very well occur, if Abigail could only be persuaded to cooperate.

But if not, if her plan failed to materialize, there was always Freddie Freyhuysing in the wings, a perfectly acceptable compromise. A satisfied smile played at the corners of her lips. How wonderful it would be, she was thinking, to have Abigail safely married and to be free of all the responsibilities and petty arguments that seemed to so frequently occur.

"A penny for your thoughts," Abigail said slyly.

Clarissa was annoyed to find herself blushing, quite certain that Abigail Worth had accurately guessed her thoughts. Infuriated, she ignored the question, thankful to see that they were approaching the lake. Since many of the members of the procession would remain to enjoy a steamer ride on the placid waters or to linger for a while at Moon's Lake House, there would be fewer vehicles on the return journey and they should reach the Pomeroys by four o'clock, precisely the correct hour for tea.

Impressive iron gates marked the entrance to the Pomeroy estate, and they had been flung open on this hot August afternoon to welcome the expected guests.

A wide dirt road, bordered by ancient elms, led straight to the house, about five-hundred yards ahead of them. As the victoria rolled along, the horses' hooves causing little clouds of dust, Abigail admired the seemingly limitless stretches of green lawns and wondered where the farmhouse and pasture lands could be. Probably so far away I'll never see them, she decided, her hope for a brief glimpse of her new acquaintance rapidly diminishing.

As they drew alongside the main house she was enthralled by the sheer beauty of it. There were no gargoyles or jutting balconies to destroy its classic lines. It was brick, the walls covered with ivy, while slender marble columns stretched to the second floor. The entrance was a half-moon shape, its floor composed of rose-colored bricks. The white double doors stood ajar, with narrow mullioned windows on either side and a fanlight above.

"Stunning," Abigail murmured.

Clarissa Worth stiffened. "I much prefer the architecture of our place," she answered as she rose gracefully to her feet, stretching out her hand to a liveried servant, leaning on him lightly for assistance as she descended to the ground.

The hallway with its marble floor was cool and dim, but as they followed the butler to the drawing room, the sunlight spilled through the open glass doors and Abigail caught a glimpse of a brick terrace bright with huge tubs of begonias.

The parquet floors glistened, the chairs and sofas were covered in stark white, while the walls, a crimson damask, provided a startling contrast.

Mrs. Archibald Pomeroy II, wearing a lilac chiffon gown, rose from a couch by the hearth to greet her guests, and Abigail, to her dismay, saw Freddie Freyhuysing and his mother seated in deep wing chairs nearby. Mrs. Freyhuysing, an enormous woman, was already demolishing a tray of sandwiches that had been placed by her side. Next to her sat Freddie, appearing, if it were possible, even more pallid and mouselike than usual.

As Abigail approached he stood up hurriedly, almost upsetting his cup of tea. "Awfully good to see you, Abigail," he muttered, blushing fiercely.

Bestowing her most dazzling smile on him, Abigail observed that he was in the process of growing a moustache and fighting a losing battle, for it was pathetically wispy and sparse. He was dressed in a white linen suit with a red carnation in his buttonhole, which failed completely to give him a rakish air, if that was what he had hoped to accomplish.

Abigail clasped Mrs. Pomeroy's outstretched hand, which was cool and firm to the touch, and found herself being guided to the sofa by her hostess and being offered a cup of tea.

"My dear," Mrs. Pomeroy murmured in a low voice. "Did you know I was a close friend of your mother?"

Abigail shook her head slowly, finding herself completely under the spell of this willowy, amazingly beautiful woman with the warmest, most intuitive brown eyes she had ever encountered.

"Someday soon you must come here alone so I can tell you about her." Mrs. Pomeroy almost whispered the words as she poured cups of tea for the newly arrived guests and refilled Mrs. Freyhuysing's empty cup.

Clarissa Worth bit daintily into a cucumber sandwich. "Are we not to meet your son?" she asked smoothly. "I've heard so many glowing reports regarding him."

Another ambitious mother with a marriageable daughter on her hands, Mrs. Pomeroy thought as she gave her guest a smile of regret. "Unfortunately not. He's remaining in London for the Season and I shall miss him quite dreadfully."

So it was not Archibald Pomeroy who I met this morning after all, Abigail thought, an expression of amusement flitting across her face as she watched her stepmother struggle to conceal her disappointment.

Freddie Freyhuysing cleared his throat nervously, remarking that as it was such glorious weather, he was looking forward to some tennis the following morning. "How about it, Abigail?" he asked, and she proceeded to accept the invitation, believing it to be the lesser of two evils—preferable to the daily trip to Congress Spring.

The conversation swirled smoothly around her, the bulk of it going in one ear and out the other, as it was mainly concerned with the Saratoga Season which to her seemed very much the same year after year.

Clarissa Worth was relieved to learn that Victor Herbert, with his fifty-four-piece orchestra was returning to the Grand Union. "I saw *Prince Ananias* four times in New York this winter," she exclaimed, "and I wouldn't mind seeing it again."

"Poor man," Mrs. Freyhuysing chimed in mournfully. "He is invariably unlucky at gambling, and I understand he's at the tables more often than not. His losses are said to be very heavy. I for one am in favor of this movement to close down all games of chance in Saratoga. I think it is a very bad influence on our young people."

"Oh, I don't know," Freddie interjected, blushing furiously when he realized he was criticizing the indomitable matriarch of the Freyhuysing household. "The men say Herbert obtains great pleasure from it and, after all, most of the people who gamble can well afford to lose."

His mother gave him a frosty look before moving on to another subject. "Well, I for one," she continued, "am in favor of seeing a certain element in Saratoga eliminated."

"Who for instance?" Abigail asked, her curiosity finally aroused.

Mrs. Freyhuysing, noted for her proclivity toward ostentation, pointed out that she objected to the presence of Diamond Jim Brady in the community, and that she considered it extremely poor taste for him to present Miss Russell with a gold-plated bicycle, her initials studded in diamonds and emeralds on the handlebars.

"Dreadful people," she said, shuddering. "And I prefer not to investigate their murky backgrounds. After all, we can't afford to have Saratoga gain a reputation for vulgarity." Selecting a heavily frosted cake from a nearby tray, she sat back in her chair, her small, beady eyes snapping with indignation.

Mrs. Pomeroy, who was well aware that Mr. Freyhuysing had made his fortune in beer, suppressed a smile. "But hasn't it already?" she asked gently as she watched the flash of jewelry on Mrs. Freyhuysing's pudgy fingers. "And isn't that what makes the season here so much fun? Heaven knows the Puritan influence in America has struggled hard enough to win out in Saratoga, and I for one am glad to say it has so far lost. Without the Diamond Jims and the Bet-a-Million Gates, Saratoga would lose its personality and become like any other watering spot."

The trays of sandwiches and cakes had been replenished and consumed. It was time to leave, and as Abigail rose to thank Mrs. Pomeroy for a lovely time, she found herself saying "You have a farm on your property too, Mrs. Pomeroy?"

"Oh, yes, a working farm that provides us with all our vegetables." She gave Abigail a curious glance. "Are you interested in farming, Miss Worth?" she asked.

"Very much." Abigail paused, unsure of what to say next but was saved from framing another question when Mrs. Pomeroy continued. "We have a very competent tenant farmer who takes such good care of the place we never have to give it a thought. He's Irish, as with the name of Sullivan you might guess, with a large brood of sons and daughters who help him considerably."

"Is one a writer?" Abigail asked breathlessly.

Mrs. Pomeroy looked puzzled again as she shook her head. "No, not that I'm aware of, but it's possible, of course."

She walked with them to the entrance and stood there waving her hand gracefully as their carriages moved off.

"A very enjoyable interlude," Clarissa commented, "except that I was most disappointed not to meet the son."

When Abigail did not reply, she gave her an impatient look. "I don't think I'll ever understand you, Abigail," she said crossly. "Whatever got you on the subject of farming?"

"Because it's a very important part of our existence, although we tend to ignore the fact," Abigail replied. "So I wanted to find out if they were putting all that acreage to good use."

"Well, at least you're playing tennis with Freddie tomorrow," her stepmother remarked, thoroughly disinterested in continuing a discussion on agriculture. "In addition, there's no question but he'll ask you to the hops and balls to which the young people are invited."

"Without question," Abigail murmured as they drove the rest of the way home in silence.

So his name is "Sullivan," Abigail was thinking, *and I was wrong in imagining he might be Archibald Pomeroy*. She too, like her stepmother, was disappointed, for she recognized that even a nodding acquaintanceship with a farmer's son would be considered by everyone she knew as beyond the pale, and the chance of it developing into a friendship or a love affair was nonexistent.

Nevertheless she continued to dream about him, curious as to what his first name could be and determined to ask him when she rode out to meet him in the morning. For, despite recognizing the impossibility of any future together, it never crossed Abigail's mind to avoid another encounter.

Chapter Four

Dinner at the Pomeroys' was always formal, whether they had guests or dined alone, and Edwina Pomeroy, glancing down the vast expanse of the highly polished table, noted with approval that her son, dashing in his evening clothes, was acquiring a tan and seemed to be thoroughly relaxed and content.

"A satisfactory day?" she inquired, smiling at him across the candlelight.

"Extremely—I finished the first chapter, a rough draft, but it seems to be going reasonably well."

"And your subject—I've forgotten to ask."

"A social history of nineteenth-century England, but not the upper classes. Rather I'm concentrating on the sadly neglected poor."

Mrs. Pomeroy gave him a gentle smile. *Ah, the very young,* she thought, *eager for a time to right the wrongs of the world before becoming smothered by the deeply rooted customs and mores of their particular social group.* As she gazed at her son she recalled this afternoon and Abigail Worth's breathless questions about the farm. Now, there was a girl quite different from the usual debutante—a girl who had obviously been completely disinterested in the frivolous teatime chatter. Mrs. Pomeroy wondered if she, too, like so many others, would in the end become the victim of her environment and marry someone like the vacuous Freddie Freyhuysing. To her surprise she found herself fervently hoping that this would not be the case.

"I met a particularly charming girl today," she began. "She came to tea with her stepmother."

Archibald laughed and raised his hand in protest. "Now, Mother, no matchmaking. Remember, you promised."

"But she was very unusual. She asked questions about the farm."

"Probably she thinks she's Marie Antoinette masquerading as a milkmaid."

"Not all young girls are silly and empty-headed," Edwina Pomeroy replied with some heat.

Her son raised his eyebrows in mild astonishment. It was unlike his well-bred mother to pick up the gauntlet for a cause, particularly at the dinner table. "What's her name?" he asked casually.

"Abigail—Abigail Worth. She's very much like

her mother. We attended Farmington together. But that was long ago." Mrs. Pomeroy sighed as memories of some of their madcap adventures, which she had not thought of in years, suddenly flooded her mind.

"Does she have unruly black hair by any chance?" Archibald asked.

"Her hair is black, yes, but it certainly wasn't unruly this afternoon. In fact she was impeccably dressed. But why do you ask? Have you met her?"

"Yes, I believe I have."

"I thought we agreed last night that you were to remain here in hiding, but if you've changed your mind, I could easily arrange to invite the Worths for dinner."

"Oh, no—that would spoil everything," her son said hastily. "You see, she thinks I'm—" He paused on the verge of describing their early morning meeting and then, quickly deciding it would be more amusing to keep it a secret, he finished rather lamely, "She doesn't know who I am."

"I see," Edwina Pomeroy said, not seeing or understanding at all.

"I feel sorry for Abigail," she added, determined to keep the subject open for as long as possible."

"Why sorry?" he asked.

Realizing she had aroused his curiosity, she

continued onward. "For one thing her stepmother is a very vapid woman, with all the earmarks of being determined to push a young girl into an early marriage."

He shrugged his shoulders indifferently. "If the girl has any character, she'll refuse to be hoodwinked."

"That's so easy for a man to say," his mother replied, finding herself becoming impatient once more with Archibald's tendency toward smugness. "Men have many options, while girls of Abigail's type do not. They are expected to marry, and far too often the choice of an acceptable husband is extremely limited."

"Ursula refused to be trapped," he replied staunchly. "Her parents had selected a very stuffy, middle-aged gentleman for her, with only one qualification as far as she could see—an impressive title. She simply declined to go along."

"Because she fell in love with you?" Edwina Pomeroy asked.

"What Ursula and I share together is much more durable than love," he explained, exasperated that his mother was still a victim of the ridiculous notion that romantic love was the most important ingredient in a marriage. "Really, Mother, sometimes I consider you the most mature woman I have ever known until you ask such utterly naive questions. This little Abigail Worth, for example, may be completely entrancing, but how long would that last? With Ursula I am assured that five, ten years from now we will continue to have as much in common as we do today."

"I see," Mrs. Pomeroy said again, recognizing by the stubborn set of her son's chin that as far as he was concerned the matter was closed and no amount of poking or prying on her part would reopen the subject. It would be futile for her to attempt to explain that a combination of love and similar interests was not out of the realm of possibility and was a giant step on the way to happiness, while a marriage without romance usually disintegrated into a bleak and sterile existence.

As they moved into the drawing room for after-dinner coffee, she conceded that she had come up against a blank wall and nothing she said or did would prevent Archibald from marrying Lady Ursula Huntington—unless Abigail Worth, who she considered fascinating, managed miraculously to convince her erudite son that falling in love was far too delightful an experience to go through life avoiding.

Chapter Five

When Archibald Pomeroy arrived at what he was beginning to call "the rendezvous," he found Abigail already there. Although she was wearing the same peculiar outfit of the previous day, this time her hair was well brushed and neatly held back from her face with a black velvet ribbon.

She certainly gives promise of becoming a beauty, he decided—her skin white and luminous, her eyes a deep cobalt-blue, her features finely cut from her patrician nose to her lips, which were sweetly curved and as red as a ripe apple.

"So you managed it again," he exclaimed.

She was sitting on the same boulder she had occupied the day before and she gave him an impish smile as he approached. "I was almost found out yesterday, but fortunately the cook likes me and promised not to tattle."

He settled down on the grassy bank, notebook and pencil in hand. "Now," he said, "we mustn't waste a moment, for I hope you have something of interest to tell me."

She giggled. "Wait until you hear! Yesterday I accompanied Mrs. Worth to Congress Spring, and in the pavilion as she and her acquaintances sipped that repulsive water, I learned the details of the most exciting piece of scandal of this season or probably any other season. Shall I describe it to you?"

"Please do—word for word as you heard it, without any embellishments."

She smiled. "No embellishments are necessary. Now here is the picture. You don't mind if I tell it as if it were taking place this very second? It's much more realistic that way."

"Not at all—carry on."

"Mrs. Horace Vandermark is sitting in her usual chair on the piazza of the United States Hotel. It is considered the best chair to occupy, for it is situated close to the piazza steps, affording her an unobstructed view of Broadway and all of the arrivals and departures.

"She is surrounded by a large group of admirers who applaud every word she utters. If she were to say, for example, that this morning the sky is green, not blue, they would enthusiastically agree.

"All is peaceful and quiet on the piazza until a smart landau moves into sight and she is startled, to say the least, to see her dutiful son, Horace, who all these years has remained a bachelor and who she fully intends to keep that way, holding the reins with a simply gorgeous girl seated beside him.

"She is deeply disturbed by his manner, for he appears neither cowed nor bewildered. Instead he is holding on to the reins with a confidence and bravado she has never witnessed before. A slight titter ripples the air around her, a titter that is instantly quelled when the ladies see the expression on Mrs. Vandermark's face.

"Gallantly Horace descends the steps of the landau, stretching out his hands to assist his companion. Her golden hair falls around her face like a shimmering cloud as she gracefully closes her lace parasol and the August sun blesses her with its rays.

"She is smiling at Horace with equal adoration and he is so bemused by her smile that he continues to stand, arms outstretched, totally oblivious to the restless prancing of the horses.

"'Horace!' Mrs. Vandermark calls out in her loud, trumpeting voice, which has been known to arouse terror in the breasts of even her most formidable opponents. And when her son does not answer, in fact does not seem to notice his mother's presence on the piazza, she rises slowly with great dignity, only two spots of color on her faded cheeks betraying her agitation, as with a toss of her head she begins her morning promenade.

"You see, what makes it all so hilarious is that Mrs. Vandermark, for the first time in her life, has found herself completely outmaneuvered. She knows now that she lingered far too long at Bar Harbor, foolishly discounting as idle gossip words of warning from her friends.

"And like an ancient tigress who has lost her teeth, she is without a weapon to combat the situation. For this girl is not pretending she is something she is not. There is no seamy reputation to unearth and expose to her son, Horace. Although the girl is obviously an adventuress—of that Mrs. Vandermark is certain—her plan has been so cleverly executed that there is nothing the old lady can do to destroy it.

"She admits to being a farmer's daughter. She admits to being penniless. She admits being forced to find employment, and after supper every evening as she plays the piano with the orchestra, her long graceful fingers lovingly stroking the ivory keys, she is the epitome of what every man in the room hungers for—a beautiful, helpless female adrift in a den of rogues, a little woman who needs protection.

"The fact that she has made it abundantly clear that she has selected Horace Vandermark as her protector has changed him overnight from a mama's boy, hiding behind his mother's skirts, to a valiant knight in shining armor—the envy of every male guest in the United States Hotel!" She ended her tale with a dramatic bow.

Archibald whistled. "What a superb raconteur you are," he exclaimed. "I only wish you had proceeded more slowly so I could have captured every word. But tell me, Annie, I'm curious to know, how did you acquire such a remarkable vocabulary?"

Abigail stirred uncomfortably, uncertain whether or not to continue the masquerade. Finally acknowledging that he had undoubtedly not been fooled into believing she was a servant, she elected to tell the truth. "Because I'm not Mrs. Chauncey Worth's maid. I'm Abigail Worth, and now that I have confessed who I am, I think it only fair for you to do the same."

"But I have nothing to confess," he replied serenely. "And I'm not at all ashamed of being a farmer. So if you have no objections to mingling with the lower class, I can't see any reason why we shouldn't continue to see each other, naturally on a completely informal and platonic basis. Now tell me, do you have any more tidbits to pass along?"

"No," she answered, still far from convinced that he was being honest with her. "It's not that I mean to criticize your station in life, for I pride myself on being broad-minded, but it is difficult for me to believe that a farm boy would toss around such words as 'platonic' and 'informal.'"

"Which shows how little you know about me. Like Abraham Lincoln I educated myself during the long winter evenings when the snow was piled high outside, though fortunately we have more modern equipment today, and I didn't have to study by firelight. In addition, intelligence has not been ladled out solely to the upper classes. In fact I believe there are signs that it is rapidly being weighted on the side of the laboring man."

She flushed. "I wasn't doubting your intelligence, but I'm still suspicious of your story, to the point where I half expected to see you yesterday afternoon."

"You did—where?" He was gazing at her with surprise.

"I was at Mrs. Pomeroy's for tea with my stepmother, and believe it or not I had the notion you might be present too."

"Farmhands don't take time out for tea and cakes."

"I realize that, but I had the absurd notion in my head that you might be Archibald Pomeroy."

He laughed ruefully. "Would that I were."

She joined in his laughter. "My stepmother was dreadfully disappointed to learn he was in London and not expected here this season. She wants us to become acquainted."

"With matrimony in mind?"

"I'm sure that's her dearest ambition."

"And how do you react to that?"

"Entirely in the negative. I told her anyone with such a name would have to be a prig."

"Oh, I don't agree—I think Archibald Pomeroy the Third, has quite an impressive ring."

She wrinkled her nose. "By the way, what is your name?" she asked.

"Sullivan, Michael Sullivan."

"Michael Sullivan! A fine Irish name, with the red hair to go along with it. But now I must go. I can't afford to be as late as I was yesterday." She started hurriedly down the path.

"Will I see you tomorrow?" he called out.

"Yes, I'm playing tennis later this morning with Freddie Freyhuysing and his crowd, which should give me ample material for another story."

She left and he continued to sit on the bank for quite some time, the beginning of Chapter Two momentarily forgotten as he speculated as to how long it would be before Abigail Worth discovered that he was not a farm boy named Michael Sullivan but Archibald Pomeroy III, pledged to another woman.

Well, never mind about that, he told himself, *for this is merely a harmless game that we are both enjoying. She is charming and amusing and somehow a cut above the ordinary stereotyped debutante, but that's as far as it goes.* Nevertheless his conscience gave him a slight twinge as he wondered if it might not become a dangerous rather than a harmless game and if it were altogether wise to pretend to be someone you were not.

Chapter Six

The Freyhuysing mansion on Filo Street had a large area in the rear set aside for tennis with two grass courts, their white lines and nets a startling contrast to the emerald green of the lawns. There was even a miniature grandstand covered with a candy-striped awning to protect the spectators from the August sun.

Half an hour late, Abigail approached the area and saw that a doubles match was already in progress—the men looking smart and well-turned-out in white flannels, the women awkward and stiff in their voluminous skirts and starched middy blouses. Recently, before each game, she had been tempted to grab a pair of scissors and cut her skirt off at the knees, but she had never been able to muster enough courage to do so, for it was one thing to mutter under one's breath how ridiculous it was to be expected to leap about the court with so many encumbrances and another thing to actually take the plunge.

Waving to Freddie and his guests, she settled down on a bench near the court and watched them lob the ball back and forth across the net. But her mind wasn't on the game, for it was still back at Kayaderosseras Creek with Michael Sullivan. It had been great fun to relate to him the trials and tribulations of Mrs. Horace Vandermark, but she was beginning to wonder what she could possibly do for an encore. Certainly any other piece of gossip would seem tepid by comparison.

She smiled a secret smile as she recalled how handsome he had looked propped against that huge boulder, pad and pencil in hand, his hazel eyes following her dramatic gestures with amusement. She sighed, thinking how unfortunate it was that he was a farmer's son. If he were Archibald Pomeroy III, for instance, or Freddie Freyhuysing, he could be right beside her on this very bench instead of doing whatever farmers do, and her stepmother would be overjoyed if she asked him to dinner.

Instead, despite the fact that he made all the young men of her acquaintance look like cardboard copies, he was without question socially unacceptable. She wondered, as she often had in the past, why a nation that called itself a democracy had set up so many barriers. Now if Michael Sullivan managed to win a fortune at the gaming tables or the track, that would become an entirely different story and everyone would be willing to overlook his humble beginnings. But she didn't suppose he had even a nickel to wager.

The players had finished their match and a maid in uniform, with perfect timing, was crossing the lawn with a tray of lemonade and cookies.

"Whew—it's going to be a scorcher," Freddie said, dropping his racquet carelessly on the grass and joining her on the bench. "After some lemonade, how about being my partner, Abigail?"

His voice brought her abruptly back to the present. "Well, as you can see, I have my racquet with me, so I certainly intend to play," she said tartly, turning away from him to greet his other guests, disconcerted by the steadfast devotion in his eyes.

She had known all of them since childhood, for they met every August at Saratoga and during the winter months in New York. Hal Staunton, his myopic eyes shielded by thick glasses, had been one of her most frequent partners at Mr. Stedman's Thursday afternoon dancing classes. She smiled, recalling that she had believed for some time he was smitten by her charms, until one day he confessed that he raced across the floor to claim her as his partner simply because she could make faster time around the ballroom than anyone else.

"Why are you smiling, Abigail?" Sally Whitney

asked. "You look like the cat who has swallowed the canary."

"I was thinking of Mr. Stedman's dancing classes."

"Heaven forbid!" Sally shuddered. She was a plump young lady who had found the tennis match far too strenuous and was wiping the perspiration discreetly from her forehead with a delicate lace handkerchief. "Thank goodness we've finally graduated to hops and balls."

"Speaking of balls," Hortense Applegate spoke up, "as we're all attending the masquerade at the Grand Union on Friday, don't you think we should decide what to wear?"

A tall, languorous blond who could easily have qualified for one of Gibson's famous models, Hortense had long since gained the admiration of Hal Staunton, and Abigail guessed that in the very near future she would be asked to be a bridesmaid at their wedding.

As they drank their lemonade the conversation revolved around what to wear to the masquerade ball.

"I'd love to go as Lillian Russell," Sally Whitney said with a giggle. "But my mother would be horrified and would say it was far too daring."

"Your curves aren't in the right places, my pet," Hortense said carelessly and then, seeing a deep blush suffuse Sally's face, she added hurriedly,

"Not that you aren't most attractive in a more respectable way."

"I think Miss Russell is simply smashing," Abigail chimed in. "Imagine having the nerve to parade along Broadway with your Japanese spaniel wearing a one-thousand-eight-hundred-dollar collar around his neck and a leash studded with precious jewels!"

"Mother thinks she's vulgar," Freddie said mildly.

"Mrs. Pomeroy doesn't think so, and where could you find a more perfect lady?" Abigail flashed back and Freddie looked distinctly uncomfortable, knowing full well that there were layers upon layers among the upper class—families like the Worths and Pomeroys, who had wealth and distinguished ancestors and families like the Freyhuysings, overloaded with worldly goods, but whose backgrounds were tactfully overlooked.

"Now let's not argue," Hortense protested. "Let's concentrate on dredging up unusual costumes."

Abigail suddenly clapped her hands with delight. "I think I'll go as Nellie Bly," she declared, "in a loud checkered suit with a copy of the *World* in one hand and a pencil in the other."

They all laughed, for Nellie Bly had recently descended upon Saratoga and, horrified by what she had seen, had peppered her newspaper column ever since with angry articles, calling the

Springs "Our wickedest summer resort" and "The Monte Carlo of America."

"What's wrong with gambling?" Freddie asked, proud of the fact that he had recently been admitted to the upstairs rooms at Canfield's Casino. "I dropped two thousand the other night."

"How unfortunate for you that you didn't win," Abigail said frostily and Freddie reddened, suggesting, with a look of abject misery in his eyes, that perhaps it was time to resume the game of tennis.

Abigail agreed and as they lobbed the ball back and forth across the net, she was thinking about the dance on Friday night and how dreary it would be to attend it with Freddie. She began to imagine herself in Michael Sullivan's arms. He would be light on his feet, of course, and as they glided across the polished floor he would find a deserted spot, away from the lights and the laughter, where he could hold her close to him and kiss her with great tenderness. She shut her eyes and missed an easy shot.

"Sorry," she said as Freddie picked up the ball and tossed her a puzzled look. "The sun was in my eyes."

The game continued and Abigail drove another return into the net as the thought crossed her mind that they would all be wearing masks and that it would be a perfect opportunity for Michael Sullivan to appear disguised as a farmer.

Chapter Seven

Abigail Worth, like any young woman who finds herself drawn to a particular member of the opposite sex, took great care with her appearance before departing on her next early morning excursion. Discarding the corduroy knickers and casual white shirt, she was smartly turned out in a midnight-blue riding habit with a matching top hat that gave her an added air of elegance.

This time Archibald was the first to arrive and when he saw her approaching, he gave a low whistle of approval. Abigail, well aware of her dramatic entrance, walked slowly and with dignity toward him and stared down wistfully at the tumbling waters of the creek, giving him the full benefit of her perfectly proportioned profile.

"You're late," he said. "I thought perhaps you had decided not to come." He was startled to discover how important it was to him that she had finally arrived.

"It isn't easy to get dressed in this outfit. Do

you like it?" Turning slowly toward him, she found herself suddenly overcome by shyness and uncertainty.

"It's smashing, but now I feel as if we are strangers and will have to get acquainted all over again."

She laughed softly and, removing the top hat, allowed her luxuriant black hair to fall about her face.

"That's better," he said. "Much better. Now tell me what pieces of information you have managed to garner since we last met."

"Nothing very much. I played tennis yesterday morning at Freddie Freyhuysing's and the main topic of conversation was what to wear to Friday night's ball. In the afternoon we took the usual carriage ride to Saratoga Lake, with my stepmother in a foul mood because we did not lead the procession. It was all very silly—a fuss over nothing."

"Ah, yes, I've heard how important it is to be first."

"We usually are but the coachman lost out this time and as a result the poor man took a terrible drubbing."

"Tell me about this Freddie Freyhuysing. I believe you've mentioned him before."

She sat down on a boulder, spreading her full skirt carefully around her. "There's not much to tell except that he's very rich and very unattractive and my stepmother is most anxious for me to marry him."

"And will you?"

She sighed. "I expect so. What else is there for me to do? It's all so ridiculous—this matchmaking, I mean. But I'll probably go along with it in the end." She laughed wryly. "My stepmother was hoping I would meet Archibald Pomeroy when we were invited there to tea the other afternoon. You should have seen the disappointment on her face when she learned he was in London and had no intention of coming to Saratoga for the Season. But it didn't matter one way or the other to me, for I imagine he's no different from Freddie."

"Would she have preferred this Pomeroy chap over Freddie?" he asked.

"Oh, yes, most assuredly, for he's not only richer than Freddie but he is also the son of an ambassador, and that would sound most impressive when the engagement was announced. But he isn't here and she can't very well inveigle him to come, so Freddie remains on the top of the list."

"But you don't love him?"

She flinched. "No, I don't love him. Yet I play tennis with him and I'm going to the ball with him on Friday. I imagine the next time he proposes I'll say yes."

"So he has already proposed?"

"Several times."

"Maybe he'll grow tired of being rejected and give up."

"Not a chance—Freddie knows he'll eventually win out and furthermore he's the type of person you simply can't insult. Have you ever known anyone like that? It's terribly frustrating. But I suppose once we are married at least I'll have some independence and be free of my stepmother."

"But you'll inherit a mother-in-law."

"Yes, and a very obnoxious one at that. But if you feed her lots of cakes and tea, she's too busy eating to interfere."

"She sounds repulsive."

"Simply revolting. But I don't want to talk anymore about Freddie, or his mother or my stepmother either for that matter."

"Fine—what shall we talk about?"

She was smiling at him and he smiled back, finding it most difficult to remain seated on the grassy bank as he was quite unexpectedly seized by an overpowering desire to gather her into his arms—a desire, he realized, that he had never experienced in the presence of Lady Ursula Huntington.

"Let's talk about you," she suggested. "What do you do when you're not milking cows or working on your book?"

"I read a great deal."

"So do I, but don't you ever go to parties and balls?"

"Country folk don't attend balls," he explained. "We square dance sometimes in the barn with the village fiddler calling the tune."

"It sounds like great fun. Do you suppose I could attend one?"

"I fear that might prove to be difficult." She gave him a pensive look. "What's troubling you?" he asked gently.

"Don't you see? We're in two different worlds." A note of despair crept into her voice. "I can't attend a square dance with you and if we happened to meet on Broadway in Saratoga and stopped to chat, it would cause a scandal. It's a predicament I don't know how to overcome."

"Ah, yes," he agreed. "We do have a problem, but with your inventive mind, perhaps you can come up with a solution?"

She was silent for a few moments, deep in thought, frowning slightly, and then suddenly she bestowed on him the most brilliant, triumphant smile he had ever received.

"I knew you'd think of something," he said.

"Yes, and it's really very simple and absolutely foolproof. We'll go on a picnic to the lake. We'll leave in the morning when everyone is at the springs, and we'll return after the promenade is over."

"But how do we get there?" he asked. "Walk?"

"Of course not. I can take the surrey and I can inveigle Olivia, our cook, to rustle up some sandwiches."

His eyes were twinkling. "And your stepmother—how will you handle that sticky situation?"

"If I tell her I'm going with Freddie, she'll be ecstatic."

"What if she discovers you're not?"

Abigail shrugged her shoulders with nonchalance. "Chances are she won't. I'm willing to take the risk if you are. Oh, do say yes." Her eyes were shining, her red lips parting as she waited breathlessly for his reply.

At first he was determined to refuse, to explain patiently that it was high time they halted these clandestine meetings, that he was betrothed to someone else and it wasn't fair to her or his fiancée to conceal the fact.

But as he was about to reject her scheme, he discovered to his surprise that it was impossible to do so, and that he could not bear to see the eager expression on her face wiped out by his arguments. *After all,* he thought, *what harm is there in going on a picnic with a beautiful young girl whose company you seem to be enjoying immensely?*

"All right," he said, "we'll go. I'll meet you on the road to the lake, a little beyond the Pomeroy's estate, tomorrow morning at precisely ten o'clock."

She breathed a deep sigh of happiness and stood up reluctantly, knowing it was past time for her to leave. He scrambled to his feet and guided her along the path to where her horse was tethered.

But this time, before she could vault into the saddle, he lifted her in his arms and placed her gently on Matilda's back. She leaned toward him to say good-bye and as she did their lips met in a kiss—a kiss that began cooly but soon became ardent.

"Don't go yet, Abigail," he whispered. His face was flushed and as he reached up to pull her down from her horse, she broke away from him and, like a fawn frightened by an unexplained sound in the woods, she wheeled Matilda about and galloped out of sight, leaving behind her a young gentleman who up to this moment had prided himself on his ability to engage in light love affairs and emerge from them unscathed and undisturbed.

After she had gone he remained for some time by the creek. The sparkle seemed to have gone out of the day, and he found himself longing for her return, so he could hold her close and kiss her once more. To his dismay he realized that he was in imminent danger of seeing his carefully constructed life rapidly destroyed.

He had not entered into his betrothal to Lady Ursula Huntington lightly—very certain then as he was certain now that she was the woman who would offer him what he needed and desired, a calm and peaceful existence. Not the least bit enamored by frivolous parties and balls, he knew Lady Ursula would be willing to live with him quietly in some isolated spot in England and ride to the hounds while he wrote.

And now this young slip of a girl had entered the picture, carelessly disrupting his placid existence to such an extent that he was finding it difficult if not impossible to concentrate on the social ills of nineteenth-century England. Beautiful, impulsive, and as he had learned today, passionate, she was not what he desired at all for a permanent relationship. Tempted by an almost overpowering yearning to enter into an affair, he ruled out seduction. She was far too sweet and innocent for that.

Thoroughly disgusted with the turmoil Abigail had brought into his life, he threw his notebook and pencil impatiently aside. It was futile to try to write. Scowling, he wrestled with his painful predicament and finally obtained some peace of mind when, with fervor, he promised himself that the picnic at Saratoga Lake tomorrow would be his final rendezvous with Abigail Worth.

Chapter Eight

As today she was properly dressed for riding, Abigail bypassed her father's house on her return from her early rendezvous. She knew that he would already be at the track watching My Clarissa's morning workout, after devouring a hearty meal with the stable boys, and, having no desire to face her stepmother across the breakfast table, she instead guided Matilda in the direction of the track.

Slowing the mare to a walk, she joined friends and acquaintances along the way without noticing them, as she relived the delightful interlude in the woods when she had found herself without warning in Michael Sullivan's strong arms and had been thoroughly kissed for the first time in her life. Not that she hadn't been kissed before during silly parlor games and once while skating in Central Park, but those had been meaningless kisses, lightly exchanged and immediately forgotten.

This, however, had been different, very different, and she shivered, wondering what might have happened if she had allowed him to pull her from her horse. Already she found herself half regretting that instinctively she had broken away from him and galloped off.

Could this be love? she asked herself. It was certainly something she had never experienced before except secondhand between the covers of a book. And if it were love, how would she be able to solve her predicament, for she knew that any serious relationship with a farm boy named Michael Sullivan would be out of the question.

Not even her father, who was noted for giving in to her requests, would tolerate the situation, and if he had even the slightest suspicion of her clandestine meetings, she knew she would be whisked off to Europe on the first available steamer. That seemed to be the panacea for any problem that faced the very rich.

Up until the present, Abigail had reluctantly accepted the fact that soon she would be expected to marry and she had even grown relatively accustomed to the idea that it would probably be Freddie Freyhuysing. But now, overnight, her whole outlook had dramatically changed. She had been kissed, she had been awakened, and she had an overwhelming desire to be in Michael Sullivan's arms again. *Is it possible*, she wondered, *that anyone else in the world has felt as deeply as this?* Being very young and extremely naive, she did not believe anyone could have.

Had he felt the same? That to her had become a vital question. She decided probably not, for somewhere along the line she had been told that it was different with a man, and blushing, she was fearful that he had probably considered her wanton. *I won't meet him tomorrow,* she told herself, yet the very next moment, despite her resolve never to see him again, she was visualizing what fun it would be to venture forth with him to the lake and share a few leisurely hours instead of their hurried early morning meetings.

Reaching the stables, she handed Matilda over to a groom and walked along the pathway that skirted the track, finding her father leaning against the fence, his eyes riveted on My Clarissa as she thundered by.

Stopwatch in hand, his eyes aglow, he turned to Abigail with a triumphant shout. "The best time ever! That settles it. I'm entering her in the Travers." He bestowed on his daughter an enthusiastic hug.

Linking his arm in hers, they strolled to the stables. The morning workout was over and the horses, protected by blankets, were being led by their trainers to their stalls. Enthusiastically he suggested a glass of champagne to celebrate.

"Coffee will be fine," she said. "I haven't had any breakfast."

"Nothing better than an early morning canter," he remarked, observing her riding habit. "But now have some breakfast, my dear, you must be famished." He seated her at a table and signaled to one of the waiters.

The racetrack never failed to enthrall Abigail and, despite her anxieties as she listened to her father order champagne and a hearty meal for her, she soaked in the beauty of the scene around her—the brilliant green lawns and the grandstand with its flags fluttering in the breeze, empty now but soon to be filled with noisy spectators and touts stationed under the trees urging the participants to place their bets before the race began. Money was lost and won very quickly at Saratoga and anyone who attended the Season in August soon became a victim of the sport and returned year after year.

"You have never looked more beautiful, my dear," Chauncey Worth was saying, and she saw that he had poured her some champagne and was offering it to her with a gallant gesture. "Here, drink to My Clarissa—one glass won't make you tiddly."

She smiled at him, caught up in his mood of celebration, and as she sipped the cool, sparkling liquid she said, "How could I refuse to drink to My Clarissa!?"

Her father acknowledged the toast and refilled

his glass. "Every day you remind me more and more of your mother."

Abigail shook her head in denial. "I could never be that lovely."

"Yes, she was extremely lovely but then so are you. Did I ever tell you that she and I were very much in love? Did you know that, Abigail?"

"No, you so rarely mention her, Father, and then I was very young when she died. I can't even remember seeing the two of you together, and if it weren't for the Sargent portrait of her in the drawing room, I wouldn't have the faintest idea what she looked like."

"Ah, the Sargent portrait! He captured her beauty to perfection. She sat for him the year before you were born. We thought we had everything, she and I, until you came into the world. That was the very peak of our happiness." A shadow of deep sadness crossed his face. "Tell me, are you happy, Abigail?"

Abigail laughed. "The great American dream," she replied with a touch of bitterness in her voice. "The belief that everyone must be happy."

"Clarissa is worried about you, and I am too."

Her lips twisted in a cynical smile. "Yes, Clarissa is worried all right, for fear I won't get married. I suppose I can't blame her too much for that. It must be difficult to have a stepdaughter always around the house."

He reached out and awkwardly patted her

hand. "You don't have to get married, you know—not unless you want to."

"What else do you suggest?"

He cleared his throat. "A trip to Europe perhaps?"

She looked at him and saw great compassion for her in his eyes. "The cure for all misery," she said gently. "But no thank you. And don't worry about me, Father. I'll be all right. I've been told young girls can be very tiresome and I guess I certainly qualify."

"You're not in love with Freddie?"

"No—not one bit."

"I suspected as much. Is there somebody else?"

It was the closest moment she had ever spent with him, and she was on the verge of telling him about Michael Sullivan, half hoping that perhaps he would understand. But the temptation to unburden her heart was only a fleeting one, vanishing at its inception, for she had lived too long in her father's world to have the slightest confidence that he would approve of his daughter breaking the rigid code that he had been taught to obey since birth. "A farmer!" he would exclaim. "My daughter meeting secretly with a farmer, and only a tenant farmer at that!" To protect her and his family from scandal, he would make sure that she was never given a chance to see Michael Sullivan again.

So instead she merely replied, "No—there's nobody else, but perhaps before I say yes to Freddie somebody more attractive will come along."

"Good girl," he said brusquely, obviously relieved by her change in mood. "I've always admired your spirit." He poured himself another glass of champagne and launched into a lengthy discussion of why he believed My Clarissa would win the Travers hands down.

Chapter Nine

It was a glorious day for a picnic and Abigail was convinced that it was a good omen and that nothing could possibly intervene to spoil her delightful plan.

At the breakfast table she mentioned demurely to her stepmother that she and Freddie were embarking on a picnic and Clarissa Worth positively beamed with pleasure. Even the normally suspicious Olivia accepted her request for a very special picnic lunch without raising one uncomfortable question. And when she asked her father if she could take out the surrey, he said, "Of course, my dear, it's high time you and Freddie enjoyed each other's company."

So with clear sailing ahead she spent a good share of the morning dressing with great care, selecting a delicate rose voile gown to wear with a large picture hat of the identical color to frame her lovely face.

Turning and twisting in front of her mirror, she

was eventually satisfied that Michael Sullivan would take one look at her and decide their adventure was extremely worthwhile despite the risk. As it was far too spectacular a day for worrying about the tomorrows, she left the house determined to savor every second of the next few hours, without allowing any doubts or fears about the future to distill her high spirits.

She had selected the perfect time for their picnic. Broadway was crowded with carriages and pedestrians hurrying toward the springs, but once she reached the dirt road leading to the lake, she passed only a single farm wagon rumbling along on its way to the village, loaded with fruit and vegetables.

Michael Sullivan was already awaiting her arrival at the designated spot, wearing an obviously new tan corduroy suit, probably his Sunday best, and this time boots that were highly polished. She could see that he too had dressed with particular care for the occasion.

She relinquished the reins to him as he climbed up beside her, and they started down the winding country road at a brisk pace between fields of tall corn stirring gently in the summer breeze.

"Olivia outdid herself," she told him with a smile. "She even slipped in a bottle of wine along with a goodly supply of sandwiches. My stepmother was elated to think that Freddie and I wanted to be a twosome and my father said 'Of course, my dear, by all means take the surrey.'"

"And you didn't have the slightest twinge of conscience?" her companion asked.

"Not the slightest. But what about your family? What did you say to them?"

"For me, it was not so complicated. I merely told them I was taking the day off."

As he turned off the main thoroughfare and followed a narrow path which led into the woods, they caught their first glimpse of the lake, shimmering in the sunlight. It was cool and damp among the trees and a welcome change from the glare of the sun.

"I know the perfect place," he said. "It's a tiny cove. I've gone there often to fish. You know, I'm sorry I didn't bring along my rod and reel."

"I'm glad you didn't, for I suspect you'd have insisted I say not one word for fear I'd disturb you. Now I've been wishing we had brought bathing attire. It's a wonderful day for a swim, or at the very least I should have worn my father's knickers so I could have waded in the shallow water."

"That reminds me of our first encounter when you burst through the thicket in that most unusual outfit." His eyes were crinkling in amusement. "But I'm glad you forgot the knickers, for what you are wearing today is vastly more becoming."

"I took particular pains to look my best, so you

see what a positive effect you are having on me. Why, in no time at all, I'll become proper and sedate and a perfect lady—exactly what my stepmother has been trying so desperately to achieve, except, I fear, she would thoroughly disapprove of the reason for my improvement."

He had halted the surrey in a small clearing and, after tying the horse to a pine tree, lifted her easily to the ground. "Don't change," he said quickly. "I want to remember you just as you are right now, at this very moment."

She had been smiling up at him until she saw that he had become deadly serious. "You sound," she said, "as if this might be the last time we'll see each other. Can't we pretend, if only for a few hours, that this will last forever?"

As he saw that her lower lip was trembling and her cobalt-blue eyes were filled with tears, he slipped his arms around her slender waist and kissed her tenderly on the forehead.

"Only on the forehead?" she asked, greatly disappointed as he turned abruptly away from her and reached for the picnic basket. "I enjoyed yesterday's kiss much more."

"But if you recall, you were frightened and ran away from me. I don't intend to have that occur today."

They had reached the little cove, and as he placed the picnic basket in the shade of a fir tree, he saw that she was pouting like a small child who has been unjustly reprimanded. "You are very young, Abigail," he said with gentleness. "And I'm sure you are aware that you are extremely lovely. Have you no conception of what a dangerous combination that could be?"

"I only know that I have never been kissed like that before and I've been dreaming about it ever since."

"You're incorrigible," he replied. "It's easy to see that associating with the Freddie Freyhuysings of this world has taught you very little about men."

"Tell me about men," she said saucily, finding a comfortable spot on the bank and sinking gracefully to the ground. "I find the subject fascinating."

He sat down some distance away from her, trying to remain serious but unable to do so. "You are a minx and what some men call a tease," he said with a grin. "And I fear if you continue on this course, you'll find yourself in all kinds of trouble. You're lucky to be here with me today instead of with some other man who mightn't be so considerate."

"I know that—you don't have to tell me how lucky I am to be here with you rather than with Freddie or any other boy I could mention."

"That isn't what I meant. You see, I could never take advantage of you, Abigail."

"Why not? Is it because you fail to find me attractive enough?"

"There you go," he said plaintively, "insisting on twisting my words. You know very well I find you attractive, and I'm sure you also know I'm tempted, very tempted, to hold you in my arms as I wanted to do yesterday."

"But you're not going to?"

"No—I'm not going to." She could tell by the stubborn set of his chin that even if she employed every womanly wile that she could muster, he would not change his mind.

"Well," she said, "in that case, as I'm starved, let's eat." Moving to the picnic basket, she knelt down and began to take out their lunch.

"You're absolutely right, of course," she said, looking up at him with a mischievous grin. "If you kissed me again today as you did before, I would run away and then you'd be faced with a dreadfully long, hot walk back to your farm. I may be impulsive, but although part of me wants to be wanton, I guess I could never go through with it."

She spread out a white tablecloth on the ground and handed him a sandwich. Their fingers touching, she gave him a sad, wistful smile. "Why must life be so complicated?" she asked.

"Only if we make it so," he replied. "Romantic love, as it is sometimes called, is a very tiresome state to be in, Abigail. You'll find that out some day very soon and be glad, very glad, that you escaped."

"How have you discovered that?" she asked in a challenging tone.

"I'm twenty-five," he replied stiffly. "I've tried it several times and believe me it's more of a mirage than reality. So, you see, by following my sage advice, you'll avoid all kinds of pitfalls and disappointments."

"Pooh," she exclaimed. "I don't agree and besides, if you've tried it several times and survived, why not risk once more with me?" Her eyes were dancing as she stretched out a slender hand, inviting him to join her on the grassy bank.

It took every bit of his resolve to resist her. Avoiding her eyes, he stood up and became very busy gathering up the remains of their picnic lunch.

"What kind of a girl do you expect to marry?" she persisted.

"One who is sober and serious and purposeful—not pretty, because that would only distract me, and above all she must shun flirtations like the plague." He frowned as he realized that unwittingly he had sketched a very accurate picture of Lady Ursula Huntington, which he feared she would consider far from flattering.

"What a shame," Abigail burst out, "that someone like Freddie is attracted to me while I'm attracted to you and you are attracted to someone who sounds as if she might be a very good match for Freddie!"

"I've already admitted I'm attracted to you," he said, struggling once more to conceal his growing desire to sweep her into his arms. "But I'm growing bored discussing the subject when there are so many more stimulating topics to occupy our minds."

"Safer topics," she said, tossing him a reproachful glance, and he knew she did not believe him, and the more he turned over his advice to her in his mind, the more he began to wonder if he himself believed what he had said.

Finally convinced that a further discussion of love would only serve to annoy him, she regaled him with tales of Saratoga, past and present, which had been handed down by her grandfather to her father and then on to her.

"You never finished telling me about Horace Vandermark," he admonished, sipping the rosé wine that Olivia had packed for the occasion, hoping the tale of Horace would help him stop thinking how entrancing Abigail looked, seated on the grassy bank near the lake, her bouffant gown spread out around her with only the tips of her satin slippers peeking out from under the hem.

"No one knows as yet what might happen," she answered, a dreamy look in her eyes. "But I'm betting on Horace winning the girl in the end. It's too bad though he isn't like you—dashing and handsome. It's difficult to imagine a great romance when the man is small and wispy and inclined to stammer."

He was smiling at her, flattered despite himself to learn that she classified him as dashing and handsome.

"Looks can be very deceiving," he replied, determined to keep their conversation on a light, impersonal note, fearful of what might occur if they failed to do so. "In your eyes I may appear dashing but actually I'm—"

"Sober, serious, and purposeful," she broke in with a grin.

Later, when the position of the sun told them it was time to leave, they returned to the surrey, driving along the country road in comfortable silence. When he reached the beginning of the Pomeroy estate, he brought the horse to a halt. They sat close together on the cushioned seat, reluctant to bid each other good bye.

"I'll see you tomorrow?" she asked. "Same time, same place?"

When he simply said good-bye and swung to the ground, she called out to him urgently. "Michael, wait a moment, there's something I forgot to tell you."

He was halfway across the road when he paused, waiting for her to continue.

"I can understand," she said soberly, "why you

hesitate to meet me again alone. I'm not as childish as you think. But there's a dance tomorrow night at the Grand Union—a masquerade ball. There'll be music in the garden. It's a very secluded spot. Won't you risk it and come? We've never danced together."

He walked back and stood by the surrey, looking up at her with that stubborn expression on his face that she was beginning to find familiar, and her heart sank as he shook his head firmly. "A farmer at the Grand Union—no, that could never be."

"On the contrary, I think it would be a lark," she protested. "Besides, if you are really serious about becoming acquainted with Saratoga society, it would be a splendid chance, for everybody will be there."

"It sounds intriguing."

"Please come."

"All right—I'll come. I promise."

Swiftly she bent down and kissed him lightly on the lips, her mood changing from despair to sheer delight. She watched him as he walked slowly down the country lane that led to the farmhouse, and it was not until he had disappeared from view, that she picked up the reins and followed the dusty road toward Saratoga, happy that she had attained one small triumph. Although he had made it clear he had no intention of seeing her again alone, she had no doubt but that he would keep his promise to dance with her tomorrow night at the ball.

I suppose I'll forget him eventually, she mused, *for I've been told often enough that time heals all wounds. Also I suppose he's right when he says romantic love is ephemeral and foolish, but I'll never be sorry we met, despite the painful moments, despite the fact that this appears to be a relationship with no future, with an ending anything but joyful.*

She knew she would miss him dreadfully for a long, long time, but nevertheless it still seemed to her to be worthwhile, no matter what the outcome, to have spent a summer's afternoon with such a man. She smiled a sad smile, finding in retrospect that she was regretful her virtue was still intact.

Chapter Ten

He was not at Kayaderosseras Creek the next morning. She had ridden there knowing in her heart that he would not come, that he had meant it when yesterday he had said his terse good-bye.

She sat there for a long while on the grassy bank, closing her eyes, leaning against his favorite boulder, imagining that he was by her side—this time miraculously with no barriers between them, with no silly arguments about the importance of love, but just the two of them savoring the prospect of a long and happy life together.

But, of course, he did not come, so eventually she rode home, spending the balance of the day being studiously polite to her stepmother and puzzling over what she would wear to the ball. For now that he had promised to attend, it suddenly became most important that she be so beautiful that although they might never meet again, he would always remember her and their first and last dance together.

She knew that most of the women who were attending had been planning their costumes ever since the announcement that this ball would be a masquerade. Some had even journeyed to New York for special fittings and others had ransacked the smart shops along Broadway in Saratoga.

Her stepmother had told her that she was appearing as Marie Antoinette, her gown an elaborate gold lamé, and the priceless diamond tiara and necklace that had been in the Worth family for several generations was being removed from the bank vault for the occasion.

To Abigail it seemed ingenious to concentrate on simplicity instead of splendor, so she selected a gown from her wardrobe that she had never worn before. It was stark white with accordion pleats from the neck to the hemline, its only decoration a narrow gold belt. With gold slippers and a matching ribbon for her hair, she planned to appear as a Greek goddess.

In the afternoon Hortense Applegate dropped by and, as it was a glorious day, they strolled through the garden and had lemonade and cookies served to them in the gazebo.

"Do you realize you passed right by me this morning without as much as a smile or a nod?" Hortense asked, giving Abigail a reproachful look.

"Really? Do forgive me. I didn't mean to be rude."

"You were in another world," Hortense continued. "In fact you've been that way every time I've seen you lately. The other day Freddie had to ask you three times if you would go with him to the ball before you came out of your trance and accepted."

Abigail grinned. "Well, I never listen very closely to what Freddie says."

"Poor fellow—I feel sorry for him. He's so hopelessly in love, and it's not fair of you to treat him in such a cavalier manner."

At her words, it struck Abigail forcibly for the first time that Freddie should not be looked upon by her as an object of derision but rather an object of pity. Having never before been exposed to the vagaries of falling in love, she had not, up until now, had the least conception of how devastating it could be to face possible rejection. And if Freddie had been suffering as she had, she had nothing but sympathy to offer him now.

"It's just that I'm not in love with Freddie," she said softly. "Tell me, are you in love with Hal?"

Hortense munched on a cookie thoughtfully. "Well, let's say," she finally replied, "that I'm comfortable with him. I certainly don't feel any wild passion. But we do have the same background, the same tastes, and I believe that's dreadfully important."

Abigail stirred restlessly in her chair. "But that's not enough—not for me anyway. I'm beginning to realize one's youth goes by very rapidly, far too rapidly, and it's a crime to squander it. Hortense, do you suppose the day will ever come when girls like you and me will be able to escape from the rigid, stultifying structure we inherited at birth? Doesn't it frighten you to think that ten years from now, twenty years from now, we'll be doing the very same things we are doing today? Traveling to Saratoga in August to attend the balls and the races; New York in the winter, dropping off calling cards in the afternoon and going to dinner parties and dances in the evenings, with an occasional trip to Europe thrown in to break the monotony, where, not surprisingly, we meet up with the very same people we see in Saratoga and New York."

Hortense laughed. "When you put it that way, it does sound frightening. But frankly what else could we be expected to do? We're fortunate, I think, to be born rich instead of poor. I, for one, would hate to be a shopgirl, or a nurse, or worst of all a teacher trying to cram knowledge into empty-headed young ladies who aren't the least bit interested in gaining an education."

"I suppose you're right. I suppose there are really no alternatives. Father told me recently that I should not feel I must marry Freddie, but if I don't, what else is there for me to do?"

Hortense finished her lemonade and gave Abigail a puzzled look. "You are in the doldrums today," she said, "and I refuse to join you. You're yearning for the moon when you know very well you can never reach it. It's childish to expect that life will be one big romance with the man of your dreams waiting for you in the wings."

"My father told me that he and my mother were very much in love."

"They were fortunate, but I don't believe that happens very often. Most of us have to settle for less and make the best of it. Unless, of course, we choose to go into a decline and be miserable and make everyone around us miserable too."

"But what if you do fall in love, only to discover the man is someone you cannot marry?"

"Has that happened to you?" Hortense asked bluntly.

Abigail flushed and, avoiding her friend's eyes, said quickly, "No, certainly not! I was merely speculating."

"It would be very tragic, Abigail, if that occurred," Hortense replied in a solemn tone, convinced that Abigail had fallen desperately in love with someone and completely at a loss to guess who it might be.

Then they switched to another subject, confiding to each other what they intended to wear to the masquerade ball.

Chapter Eleven

Edwina Pomeroy was a most intuitive woman, particularly as far as her son was concerned, and when he joined her in the drawing room after dinner for coffee, she became convinced that his gloomy mood was caused by one of the most universal, age-old problems—he was in the process of falling in love.

She was further convinced that as he could not possibly be in love with his fiancée, Lady Ursula Huntington, and in addition, as this mood had not descended upon him until after his arrival in Saratoga, he must have become involved with someone in the immediate neighborhood.

Summing this all up, it did not take her long to surmise it was Abigail Worth he was meeting on his early morning rides, for when she had mentioned Abigail to him one day, he had asked if she had black unruly hair. Well, Abigail's hair was certainly black and Mrs. Pomeroy could easily imagine that it was often unruly, particularly when she had been riding.

So by putting two and two together she had reached the conclusion that not only had Archibald been meeting the girl but, against his better judgment and despite a valiant effort on his part, he was finding her too attractive.

Knowing her son's unfortunate propensity toward the intellectual approach to life and his deep-seated stubbornness, plus his reluctance to ever admit he was wrong, she sensed that he must be undergoing a considerable amount of inner struggle. After all, he had committed himself to Lady Ursula, believing strongly that romantic love was nonsensical and that a man was far better off to select a mate who was his intellectual equal, who scoffed with him at sentimentality, considering the elemental forces in man's nature not only distasteful but rather ridiculous.

Yes, Edwina Pomeroy agreed silently, that was a perfect description of Lady Ursula and she found herself fervently wishing that when her son's inner struggle was finally resolved, Lady Ursula would emerge a poor second. With many years of knowledge and experience behind her, she had realized at the outset that all too soon Archibald would discover that marriage to Lady Ursula was a barren and miserable existence.

Besides, she had been immediately attracted to Abigail Worth. She was very young and immature, no doubt, but like Abigail's mother at her age, when she met and fell in love with Chauncey Worth, she had all the ingredients for becoming a warm and lovable woman with just the right amount of the madcap in her nature to keep a man bemused and befuddled long after the honeymoon was over.

Therefore, having reached the conclusion that Abigail would make her son the ideal mate and being a woman noted for taking direct action, as she poured their coffee into delicate Dresden cups she began to lay the groundwork for an extensive campaign.

First she would attempt to persuade Archibald to attend tonight's masquerade ball and, after that was accomplished, she would have a note delivered to Abigail Worth tomorrow morning asking her to come to tea that afternoon—without her stepmother.

"Is your novel going badly?" she asked her son, breaking the strained silence that had developed between them.

"Oh, no, it's coming along quite smoothly."

"But I believe you're concentrating on it far too intently," she continued, giving him a sympathetic smile. "Don't you think it might be beneficial to put it aside for at least one evening? There's a masked ball tonight at the Grand Union and it might be fun for you to attend. I understand Victor Herbert's orchestra is playing in the ballroom and another group has come up from New York to play in the garden. With a mask on and some sort of makeshift costume, there's a good chance you could enjoy yourself without being recognized."

To her great disappointment he brushed aside her suggestion and, remarking that he had a great deal of writing to accomplish, he finished his coffee and excused himself.

Alone in the great drawing room, she sadly admitted that she had undoubtedly lost the first round in her campaign. She began to regret that she had left London in July and had come to Saratoga to reopen The Elms. It had been foolish of her to think that August in Saratoga would make Archibald forget England and Lady Ursula, and, as so far her plan had been a complete failure, in retrospect she realized it would have been wiser to remain at the Embassy with her husband, giving her son free rein to work out his own destiny.

Lonely and depressed, she retired early, noticing as she climbed the stairs to the second floor that the light was still burning in Archibald's room. Tossing and turning in her bed, she was surprised much later to hear the creak of a carriage in the driveway. Getting up, she hurried to the window to see their surrey going at a fast pace down their driveway.

So he has taken my advice after all, she thought, and with a smile of deep satisfaction she returned to her bed, at last able to sleep.

Chapter Twelve

The Applegates had asked six young couples, all close friends of their daughter, Hortense, to have dinner before the ball in the restaurant of the Casino. Newly refurbished and expanded by Canfield, it was a vast and impressive European-style dining room with octagonal stained-glass windows in the vaulted ceiling creating an especially dramatic effect.

Tonight to celebrate such a gala affair the room was lit by candles and the slender white pillars, which ran the length of both sides of the room, were festooned with clusters of evergreen branches and red roses.

At the far end of the salon above the small paned windows hung the racing silks of the perennial stable owners at Saratoga—the Sanfords, the Vanderbilts, the Wideners, the Worths, and many others. While the young people enjoyed an elaborate dinner prepared by the famous French chef, Jean Columbin, chamber music provided a soothing background.

Despite the disappointments of the day, Abigail found it impossible to remain dejected in such festive surroundings. Even Freddie appeared rather dashing tonight in the costume of a pirate with a patch over one eye and a rakish black three-cornered hat. Remembering how shattering it was to be treated casually by someone you cared for, she went out of her way to be attentive, and he responded with an eagerness that bordered on the pathetic.

Dinner over, they moved on to the Grand Union. The main ballroom with its magnificent crystal chandeliers was ablaze with lights. It was a grandiose room with the 3,000-pound allegorical painting *The Genius of America* by Yvon covering one entire wall.

Everybody was there and Abigail was amused to see her stepmother, resplendent in the Worth diamonds, being escorted to the dance floor by William C. Whitney, considered by many to be the most influential man in Saratoga.

Searching and not finding her father in the crowd, she imagined he had already escaped to one of the private suites upstairs to gamble, which meant, if this were true, that tomorrow would be an uncomfortable day for every member of the Worth household as Clarissa vented her ire, starting with Abigail and descending down the line to the scullery maids.

They had put on their masks, and after circling the ballroom several times, the young people decided that this was definitely the place for the older generation and that they would find the dance floor in the interior court of the hotel far more suitable.

The garden proved to be a veritable fairyland with Japanese lanterns suspended from the trees and benches in the shadows, where couples could enjoy a delightful breeze as they sipped cool, refreshing drinks and watched the dancers glide across the highly polished floor.

At first Abigail found herself searching the crowd eagerly hoping to find Michael Sullivan there, but by eleven o'clock, thoroughly discouraged that there had been no sign of him, she begged Freddie for a brief respite, urging him to be gallant and dance with Althea Spaulding, a plain, sallow girl, the perennial wallflower, who was sitting alone in a corner of the piazza.

Weary and warm, Abigail found a vacant bench and, sitting down, was startled when she heard a voice close behind her. Whirling around, she confronted Michael Sullivan.

"I thought you had broken your promise," she said with a sharp intake of her breath.

He was in the shadows but she could see that he was wearing shabby corduroys with a large straw hat on his head, partially concealing his face.

"I never break a promise." He held out his hands to her, lifting her gently to her feet and without another word they began to dance. She had been right when she assumed he would be light on his feet. As they swayed to the rhythm of the music it seemed to her that nowhere in the world would she ever be able to find a partner who would match his steps so perfectly with hers.

The orchestra was playing Victor Herbert's latest triumph, a plaintive song of love, and as Abigail felt his arm tighten about her waist as he drew her close to him, she trembled and all of the arguments that she had marshalled since their first encounter as to why it would be best if they were to never meet again crumbled.

All too soon the music ended. He led her to a bench in the farthest corner of the garden, isolated from the crowd, with only the silvery splash of a fountain disturbing the stillness around them.

"I waited for you this morning," she said.

"I wanted to come."

"Why didn't you?"

"Because as you must know it's becoming an impossible situation." His voice was replete with sadness. There was no question in her mind that his decision to never see her again was final.

The silence around them deepened. Their shoulders were touching and soon he turned to her and, placing his hand on her chin, tipped her face back and studied it with grave intensity.

"You're amazingly beautiful," he whispered.

She smiled a tremulous smile. "That's what my father told me yesterday and at the time it did not seem too important. But tonight it makes me immeasurably happy that you think so."

"How old are you?"

"Eighteen."

"Strange, I thought you much younger."

She stiffened. "I'm not a child. Why do you always treat me as one?"

"No, you are not a child," he murmured. And drawing her to him, he kissed her full, sensuous mouth tenderly and then rested his cheek against hers.

"We mustn't meet again," he said firmly.

"And why not?" she exclaimed, determined not to accept the inevitable, as without warning her cobalt-blue eyes flashed with anger. It seemed clear to her now that they were in love and should somehow find a way to surmount the ridiculous barriers erected between them.

"Because can't you see, Abigail, it's purely a physical attraction and the element of danger when we meet has made it even more so."

"Couldn't we be falling in love?" she asked, shocked by her boldness as the words tumbled out without her volition.

"Love!" There was a tinge of cynicism in his

voice. "Perhaps you are still a child after all, Abigail. No, soon you will marry Freddie and soon I will marry—someone else, and to the both of us this will become what it really is—a charming interlude, totally without substance."

Abruptly she rose and gazed down at him, her anger replaced by scorn. "If that is what all of this means to you," she said stormily, "I agree with you and think you're absolutely right when you say we shouldn't meet again. At the picnic when you stated your silly opinions on love, I didn't take you seriously, but now I do, and if you truly feel that way, you're correct in believing we wouldn't be able to find happiness together." Turning swiftly, she ran down the garden path toward the lights and the dance floor, almost stumbling into the arms of Freddie Freyhuysing.

"Where on earth have you been, Abby?" he asked. "I've searched for you everywhere." He was staring at her with a perplexed expression and it took great effort for her to muster a serene smile.

"I was wandering through the garden," she replied cooly. "It's such a glorious evening, Freddie, I hate to have it end."

"It doesn't have to end yet, Abigail," Freddie said. "Let's take a stroll together."

"Later, but now I prefer to dance, and after that I want a glass of champagne before we dance again. You're such a comfort to me, Freddie, dear.

Do you have the least conception of what you're beginning to mean to me?" As she spoke she raised her voice so that if Michael Sullivan were anywhere nearby, he could not fail to hear every word she was saying.

Freddie Freyhuysing was staring at her, mesmerized, as an expression of great joy crossed his face. "Oh, Abby," he exclaimed, "you can't imagine how long I've been waiting for that." With an air of proud possession he took her hand and guided her toward the refreshment stand.

The rest of the evening became a blur to Abigail. She smiled, she chatted with her friends, and she flirted outrageously with Freddie. She even allowed him to kiss her at her door when she said good night, slipping inside quickly to forestall another proposal.

Grimly she climbed the stairs to her bedroom with the words "a charming interlude totally without substance" engraved indelibly in her mind. *So that is all it has meant to him,* she thought bitterly. She reached her room, slamming the door behind her and flinging herself on her bed. At last she allowed the tears to flow. Much later she dried her eyes and, dashing cold water on her face, stared at her reflection in the mirror, surprised to find that except for a slight puffiness she looked remarkably the same.

Later, much later, she undressed, but instead of climbing into bed she knelt by her window, breathing in the sweet smell of the flowers in the garden below, listening to the clop-clop of horses' hoofs as a carriage entered their deserted street. She supposed by now that Michael Sullivan was fast asleep, the evening forgotten. Clenching her fists, she vowed that as of that moment she would erase him completely from her mind, and never again would she allow any man to touch the deep chords inside her that cried out for an everlasting love affair.

Chapter Thirteen

The next morning the breakfast room at the Chauncey Worths' was saturated with a strained atmosphere teetering on the edge of a real explosion. Chauncey Worth, cognizant of his wife's displeasure and uncomfortably aware of the dangerous undercurrents swirling around him, for once decided to forgo the pleasure of immersing himself in the sporting pages of his newspaper and attempted valiantly to smooth the ruffled waters.

"Well, my dear," he said to his wife, "you were certainly a sensation at the ball last night."

Clarissa Worth tossed her head and gave him a frigid stare, refusing to be so easily mollified. "I'm surprised you noticed," she replied coldly, "since soon after we reached the Grand Union you disappeared from my sight. Really, Chauncey, it is most disheartening to have one's husband desert one for the gaming tables. At the very least you might have asked me for the first dance."

"It happens every day," Abigail broke in, expressing her new-found cynicism. "I'm surprised, Clarissa, that a woman as cosmopolitan as yourself hasn't come to that conclusion long ago."

About to turn her wrath on her stepdaughter, the situation was saved as one of the maids entered with a stack of letters and Clarissa, who avidly looked forward to the seemingly endless stream of invitations, became absorbed in studying each envelope.

"Here's one addressed to you," she said to Abigail, "from The Elms." She lifted her eyebrows, registering surprise.

"What does Mrs. Pomeroy say?" she asked as Abigail unfolded a sheet of paper tinted a pale lilac.

"She has issued me an invitation to tea—this afternoon." Abigail looked up from the letter with a bemused expression on her face until she recalled Mrs. Pomeroy informing her the other day that she and her mother had been chums at school, and that she wanted an opportunity for a quiet chat.

"She probably wants to talk to you about your mother," Chauncey remarked. "She and Abigail were always the closest of friends. As a matter of fact, Abigail was an attendant at Edwina's wedding."

"Did she fail to include me in the invitation?" Clarissa asked with some asperity.

"I'm afraid she did." Abigail folded the letter and crammed it into the pocket of her skirt, not at all certain she wanted to go anywhere near The Elms. After last night's humiliating episode she had made up her mind never to ride in the direction of Kayaderosseras Creek or the Pomeroys' estate again, knowing the memories surrounding them were far too painful to be revived.

"I suppose I'll have to go," she muttered.

"But, of course," Clarissa said as Chauncey gave Abigail a quick glance, disturbed to note how pallid and listless she appeared.

Probably too much champagne, he decided, and returning to the sports page, forgot all about the members of his family as visions of My Clarissa winning the Travers by several lengths danced before his eyes.

Edwina Pomeroy was seated at the breakfast table at The Elms, lingering over her coffee when Archibald joined her. Observing the extremely grim expression on his face, she was fearful that whatever had occurred the night before was not entirely to his liking.

"How was the ball?" she asked.

He glanced at her quizzically. "How did you know I went?"

"I heard a carriage under my window and took a wild guess. Was it enjoyable?"

"Not very—the usual noise and confusion, with

people drinking more champagne than was good for them and running around in silly costumes."

Edwina Pomeroy sighed, wondering how much longer it would be before her son would outgrow his rather supercilious attitude toward the very rich. After all, he was one of them, and she had observed that although he had spent a great deal of time since leaving Oxford sponsoring hopeless causes, he also seemed to enjoy the benefits his station in life provided—such as expensive wines, Thoroughbred horses, and memberships in the most exclusive clubs.

But she still managed to gaze at him fondly, for he was her only child and sooner or later she was confident he would outgrow this difficult period and turn out to be as charming and understanding as her dear husband.

"Oh, by the way," she said quickly as she saw he was on the point of leaving for his room and a morning of work. "I've asked someone to tea this afternoon, so you'd better be careful and remain in hiding."

"Who?" he asked idly.

"Abigail Worth."

"Why ever Abigail Worth!?" he exploded. "She was here to tea only the other day."

"I'm aware of that," Mrs. Pomeroy answered evenly, "but I found her most entrancing, and as her mother was my dearest friend, I want to have a longer chat with Abigail."

His expression softened. "Yes, she is enchanting," he admitted.

"That's right, I remember now that you mentioned you had met her."

"Oh, yes, several times."

"Then why not forget this absurd idea of yours of becoming a prisoner in your own house and join us for tea." Edwina Pomeroy's eyes were shining as she sensed she might be close to victory.

His face had clouded over. "No, I couldn't—not after last night. You called her enchanting and that she is, but she's very young and rather childish and most impulsive—one of those beautiful light-weight debutantes I'm determined to avoid at all costs."

"Yes, she would be impulsive," Edwina Pomeroy agreed, a smile playing on her lips, "if she's anything like her mother. But childish and a light-weight—I find those descriptions hard to believe."

He shrugged his shoulders. "She's the same as all the rest of them, wanting to marry her dream prince and live happily ever after in a storybook world that unfortunately does not exist."

"And what's wrong with that?" his mother snapped, finding it impossible to remain patient one second longer.

"You'd understand what I mean if you would

make an effort to become acquainted with Ursula."

Mrs. Pomeroy bit her lip, almost bursting out with "Damn Ursula," but she succeeded in not doing so and instead remarked drily, "As you intend to marry Ursula, I suspect I shall get to know her very well."

They stared at each other across the breakfast table, mother and son, both with ruffled feathers. Mrs. Pomeroy rose gracefully from her chair. "I'm growing tired of Saratoga," she said. "I miss your father and as you obviously must miss Ursula, maybe we should close the house quite soon and return to London."

"I believe we should," he agreed as they parted on a more amicable note.

Chapter Fourteen

As she drove the surrey through the gates of the Pomeroy estate and along the wide lane to the main house, Abigail Worth was oblivious to the beauty of the scene around her, concentrating valiantly on appearing before her hostess as a young, lighthearted girl without a care in the world.

Last night had been a devastating experience. Up until then she had refused to accept defeat, pinning her hopes, she now knew falsely, on her dance with him, hoping it would be the catalyst destroying once and for all the arguments he had built up in his mind against falling in love.

She had known in her heart, from the outset, that he was not a farm boy—he was far too sophisticated and cosmopolitan for that. But if not a farm boy, who could he be? She was certainly on at least a nodding acquaintance with all the young men who idled away the month of August in Saratoga, and he was definitely not one of them. She realized that Archibald Pomeroy would be the logical answer, but he was not here, he was in London.

Going full circle and coming up with no solution, by the time she halted the surrey in front of the house, she was determined to ask Mrs. Pomeroy some questions regarding Michael Sullivan and at least establish the fact, once and for all, that he was not her dashing companion at Kayaderosseras Creek.

Following the butler through the hallway to the drawing room, she found herself anxious to renew her friendship with Edwina Pomeroy and at the same time nervous, uncertain of just how she could raise questions regarding the Sullivan family without arousing curiosity.

Entering the drawing room, she found her hostess seated on a couch, awaiting her arrival. "My dear," she said stretching out her hand in greeting, "how very lovely you look today. On you rose is a most becoming color."

Abigail was wearing the same gown she had worn to what she now considered "the disastrous picnic" and as she accepted the gracious compliment with a smile she could not help but wish her escort had been as impressed.

Edwina Pomeroy patted the cushion on the sofa and Abigail joined her. "I wanted to tell you the other day," she said shyly, "how much I admire your house."

Mrs. Pomeroy busied herself pouring the tea. "When it was built over twenty years ago," she explained, "I persuaded my husband to avoid the Victorian or the Gothic. I believe architecture, particularly in the country, should be classic, with the simplest of lines."

Abigail chuckled. "You are certainly the exception in Saratoga. Our house, like so many others in the village, is a conglomeration of balconies and turrets. After it was completed my father journeyed to India and when he returned he insisted on adding a minaret. Our town house on Fifth Avenue is what I call flamboyant Gothic. I'm not even certain of the exact number of rooms, and when I was very small I was constantly losing my way and wandering up and down strange corridors."

"I know it well," Mrs. Pomeroy said, "for I visited it frequently after your mother married Chauncey. In fact I remember attending a dinner party there once when you were a baby and your mother took me up to the nursery for a peek at you. She was enormously proud of you, Abigail. It was tragic that she died so young before you had a chance to get acquainted."

"But after she died, why didn't you return?" Abigail asked.

"There were several reasons. Your father became a recluse for several years. He refused to see anyone. Later my husband joined the diplomatic service and we began our travels to distant corners of the world. It was unfortunate that over the years we lost track of many of our oldest friends."

"You will return to London soon?" Abigail asked.

"Yes, I miss my family, but I miss New York too dreadfully. Recently my husband promised me that nothing will stand in the way of our reopening our home there this winter for at least part of the Season."

"Perhaps I'll see something of you then," Abigail ventured.

"Without a doubt," Mrs. Pomeroy replied firmly. "I canceled a ball here this summer due to the absence of my husband and son, but nothing will deter me from holding one in New York and you will without question be among the invited guests."

Replenishing their teacups, she launched on a series of lively accounts of early days in New York when she was growing up and how she and Abigail's mother traced their friendship back to childhood and through the years together at Farmington.

"I married quite some time before your mother. She was an attendant at my wedding," Edwina Pomeroy continued. "You must be aware of how lovely she was both in appearance and character.

One glance at the Sargent portrait of her in your drawing room shows why she was rated a great beauty. I'm glad you have that portrait, my dear, and I trust you study it frequently. You are growing so much like her that when I first saw you the other day it brought back many precious memories."

It was growing late. Abigail hesitated to introduce the subject of Michael Sullivan but finally, straightening her shoulders and telling herself sternly not to be a ninny, she took the plunge.

"Remember," she began nervously, "you were telling me the other day about your farm and the Sullivans?"

Mrs. Pomeroy nodded her head, mystified why Abigail Worth was again showing such an interest in the subject.

"Well, does Mr. Sullivan have a son named Michael, who desires to be a writer?" Thankful to have managed to get the question out in the open, she sat tensely beside her hostess, her hands clasped tightly in her lap.

"There are three Michael Sullivans in the family, Abigail," Edwina Pomeroy replied. "The father, the head of the household, a man in the neighborhood of his sixties; his son, who has been married for some years and has one offspring, a little boy, around five or six I would say."

"And the middle Michael. How old is he?"

Mrs. Pomeroy frowned. "Oh, I'd guess thirtyish,

and if anyone has told you he's a writer, they're pulling your leg. The Sullivans are fine, upstanding people but hardly well educated. I wouldn't be surprised if all they could manage would be to sign their names."

"And he doesn't have red hair," Abigail persisted, determined to weather through to the very end.

"No—it's rather a mousy brown." Mrs. Pomeroy was about to add "But, my dear, why do you ask?" when the last piece of the puzzle, which had been troubling her for some days, fell easily into place. So Archie had been fobbing himself off as Michael Sullivan, making up such an absurd tale to conceal his identity. Her lips tightened and for the first time in her life she felt anger for her son welling up inside her. She considered it a despicable game to play with one so young and innocent.

With a great effort she succeeded in keeping her voice light. "I can't imagine where you heard that story," she said, "but then in Saratoga there are so many bits of gossip being bruited about that possibly it's not so surprising after all."

The tea hour was over. Abigail rose to her feet. "Thank you so much," she said, "for the delicious tea and, what's even more important, telling me anecdotes about my mother. I never have felt I knew her at all until today. It's extremely difficult for my father to talk about her."

"It was a pleasure." Edwina Pomeroy slipped her arm companionably around Abigail's waist and walked with her to the door. "We'll meet again soon, I promise. Remember, too, you're invited to my ball."

"Thank you, I'll surely come." Abigail was surprised and touched when her hostess kissed her lightly on both cheeks and gave her a warm hug.

Mrs. Pomeroy continued to smile and wave her hand as the surrey started down the driveway, but as soon as it had disappeared from sight, she made no effort to hide the anger that had been building up ever since Abigail's tremulous questions—deep-seated anger and displeasure at Archibald for his foolish deception and even greater anger to think that he remained bound and determined to marry Lady Ursula after someone as desirable as Abigail Worth had crossed his path. "Foolish boy!" she exclaimed and then began to ponder on how to broach the whole unpleasant subject to her son.

Chapter Fifteen

At dinner that night Edwina Pomeroy faced Archibald across the candlelit table, struggling to maintain the composure that she had attained after years of training.

Her son, who seemed totally unaware that his mother's wrath was about to descend upon him, sipped his vintage wine with great pleasure and began to discuss Chapter Three of his book.

"I'm not interested in hearing about your novel tonight, Archibald," she said coldly.

He glanced up at her in surprise, for once completely offstride, as his mother seldom failed to listen to him without giving him her undivided attention.

"Why ever not?" he exclaimed. "Do you feel ill, Mother? Maybe you've been around the house too much and should take a trip to the springs tomorrow."

"You know how I have always detested the waters," she replied. "And there's nothing wrong with my digestion. But I'm annoyed with you, Archibald. Perhaps annoyed is too bland a word. Let's say I'm enraged—totally enraged."

"Well, if you'll tell me what I've done to upset you, it would be appreciated." He spoke with maddening calmness.

His reply irritated her even more, for it reminded her of the times when her husband would refuse to become upset by some incident she considered outrageous. She wondered with sadness if the day would ever arrive when men would overcome their smug conviction that they were the superior sex, treating their women with a condescension that to her bordered on the insulting.

"Abigail Worth was here today for tea and before she left, she asked me some very probing questions about the Sullivans. It didn't take too much intelligence on my part to solve a puzzle which has been disturbing me for some time. Why in the world, Archibald, did you find it necessary to be deceitful and pretend to Abigail that you were Michael Sullivan? I've never been ashamed of you before, but I am tonight."

"It all started out in fun," he protested, beginning to feel extremely uncomfortable.

"Fun," she repeated mockingly. "What a strange definition of fun. I suppose it has never crossed your mind that you have made the poor child most unhappy." She hesitated and then added rather awkwardly, "I trust your intentions were strictly honorable."

Archie flushed. "They certainly were at the outset and when they began to border on the dishonorable, I broke it off. I assure you nothing untoward happened—nothing of which I have any reason to be ashamed."

She drew a deep breath of relief. "Let's be thankful that, as you put it, 'nothing untoward happened,' but I still question your statement that you did nothing of which you should be ashamed. When a young girl's emotions are tampered with by a man quite a bit older than she, I consider him beastly."

"Does she know now who I really am?" he asked, avoiding his mother's eyes.

"Difficult as it was for me, Archibald, I honored my promise to you and told her you were in London. But, of course, when I got through answering her questions about the Sullivans, there was no doubt in her mind, if there ever had been, that she had been duped."

He stirred restlessly in his chair and fiddled nervously with his glass of wine. "I'm sorry if it developed into such a sticky situation. I honestly didn't believe at the start that that would occur. What do you think I should do?"

Edwina Pomeroy, although relieved to see that he was suffering because of his duplicity, remained determined to give him no quarter. "I think," she stated sternly, "that the only decent thing for you to do is to go to her and tell her the truth."

"I can't see her again," he burst out. "But you're right, it's only fair to tell her the truth. I'll send her a letter."

His mother was still not appeased. "So you're not prepared to meet her face to face?"

"No—I told you I can't. I'm sorry if you are disappointed in me. A letter will simply have to suffice. Besides, we'll be closing up here soon and leaving for England, while she'll be returning to New York, where she'll be so inundated with parties and balls that our meetings here will shortly be wiped from her mind completely."

His mother continued to stare at him with an expression of deep sadness. "I wish I could be that confident," she said. "I'm afraid, my son, you don't have the vaguest conception of how dangerous and, yes, tragic it can be to meddle with a young girl's emotions. Settle for a letter, if you must, and we can only hope that the hours you shared with her, which you apparently took so lightly, will eventually be taken lightly by her too." With a proud dip of her head, Mrs. Pomeroy rose and swept out of the room.

Chapter Sixteen

The next morning in the post Abigail Worth received her letter from Archibald Pomeroy. Seeing the return address of The Elms on the envelope, she grabbed it swiftly from the pile of mail that a maid had delivered to the breakfast room and ran pell-mell out of the house and through the garden to the gazebo.

Recognizing that it was not addressed in Mrs. Pomeroy's fine script, she suspected that it was from her son and that for some reason unknown to her his mother had felt it necessary to conceal the information that he was not in London but in Saratoga. She opened it with shaking fingers and started to read. It began—

My dear Miss Worth:

I think I played the game of being a farmer too long until it became, not a game, but something more serious.

Did you suspect from the beginning that I was not Michael Sullivan? I'm certain you did.

But I don't believe you discovered my true name, for my mother honored her pledge not to reveal to anyone that I was in Saratoga.

I know now that I should have told you from the outset who I was and I also should have informed you that I am bethrothed to a girl of sterling character—Lady Ursula Huntington.

So, my dear Abigail, let us remember our few brief encounters with fondness, mixed with a dash of nostalgia, and no regrets.

                     Archibald Pomeroy

It was the word "betrothed" that was of more significance to Abigail than any other part of his letter. To learn that he had promised himself to someone else was without question the greatest blow of all. Her reactions ran from anger that he had treated her in such a cavalier manner to sadness that their "game," as he called it, was over, and to despair that there was not the slightest hope that their lives would ever touch again in a meaningful relationship.

Since their first meeting an underlying thread

of excitement, of anticipation, had possessed her from the moment she awoke in the morning until she fell asleep at night. And now suddenly the whole world became a dull, flat gray.

The sky was as blue as ever without a cloud. A soft breeze fluttered the leaves of a maple tree in the far corner of the garden. The flowers were still gay and colorful in their neat beds. But all this passed unnoticed as she sat in the gazebo, his letter slipping from her hands to the floor.

She could hear familiar sounds coming from the kitchen, the clatter of pots and pans and the clink of china as preparations for the next meal began. She heard the milkman's wagon creaking as it moved along the street and the crack of his whip as he urged his aged horse onward. Later she saw Tommy bringing the surrey out of the stables for the morning pilgrimage to Congress Spring, followed by Clarissa calling for her in a loud, exasperated voice. But all this was merely a blurred background to her turbulent thoughts.

By midmorning she had changed into her riding clothes and was cantering along the wooded trails, carefully avoiding the path that led to Kayaderosseras Creek. She rode until she was exhausted and Matilda was in a lather. Returning home, she reached her room unnoticed to fling herself on her bed dry-eyed, weary, still unable to accept the inevitable fact that to Archibald Pomeroy their meetings had been inconsequential—a lighthearted dalliance with a young and extremely naive girl, something to occupy his mind to make the days a trifle less lonely before he could gather his fiancée into his arms once more. She found herself hating with passion a woman called Lady Ursula Huntington who he had described to be of "sterling character." *Sterling character!* She wondered if by that remark he was intimating that she was not.

Admitting that perhaps she had inadvertently given the impression of being irresponsible and unreliable, she regretted that it was far too late to alter the impression.

It was dark when Olivia tapped with great urgency on her bedroom door and listlessly, with a tremendous effort, she arose and turned the key.

Bristling with anger to cover up her anxiety, Olivia entered, carrying a heavily laden tray, placing it on a table near the window. "You haven't eaten all day," she said in an accusing tone. "You have everyone in the household topsy-turvy. Whatever is the matter with you, Miss Abigail?"

Abigail crossed to her dressing table and stared at herself in the mirror. Her hair was tousled, her riding habit rumpled, and her face streaked with dust from the long gallop through the woods.

"Nothing that a hot bath and a good sleep won't cure," she said, determined not to confide to anyone, not even to Olivia, her complete and utter misery.

"Mr. Freyhuysing has called three times," Olivia continued accusingly. "Have you forgotten you were supposed to play tennis this afternoon and go to a party tonight at the Whitneys'?"

"What did you tell him?"

"I said you had a headache. He was most concerned. He has sent you red roses with his love."

"His love!" Abigail turned from the mirror, a bitter smile playing on her lips. Poor Freddie! Was he suffering as she was suffering? If so, he had her sympathy. *At least now we have one thing in common,* she thought, *if we both have learned how devastating unrequited love can be.*

"Thank you, Olivia, for being so kind," she said, and crossing to the table, she lifted the silver covers on the tray only to quickly replace them.

"I guess I'm not hungry after all."

Olivia stood by the door, her arms akimbo in her favorite stance, expressing her concern. "Miss Abigail, it's not like you to mope around. Do you think you have a fever?"

For the first time that day Abigail smiled. "No, Olivia, I'm not ill. All I need is a hot bath and some sleep. By the way, are my father and stepmother about?"

"They left for a party at the Sanfords'. Your father was most reluctant to go. He's worried too."

"Well, he needn't be." She began to remove her

riding clothes. "When they return, tell him I'm feeling much, much better. It was only a migraine. And if Freddie calls again, say I'll play tennis with him tomorrow."

"That's better," Olivia declared cheerfully.

Abigail began to brush her tousled hair with vigor. Their eyes met in the mirror and Abigail saw sympathy mixed with concern on the old cook's face.

"Don't worry, Olivia," she said gently, wondering how much she had surmised about her early morning expeditions. "I'm not going into a decline. I'm a silly, stupid girl who has learned a difficult lesson and will never be so silly and stupid again." Impulsively she turned from the mirror and gave the old cook a quick hug.

Olivia picked up the heavy tray. "Have your bath," she said, speaking brusquely to hide her emotions. "In a little while I'll bring you some hot soup."

Olivia's age-old remedy for any complaint—from a headache to a nasty cold or a broken heart—brought Abigail to the crossroads, as at last she accepted the unpleasant truth that Archibald Pomeroy, on his own volition, had chosen to step out of her life forever.

Possessing a strong character, a healthy distaste for people who were unable to face up to and solve their problems, and an enormous amount of pride, she arose early the next morning prepared to spend the day as though nothing of any significance had occurred to disrupt the even tempo of her existence.

Chapter Seventeen

As she entered the breakfast room her father looked up at her anxiously, obviously relieved when she gave him a cheerful peck on the cheek before pouring herself a cup of coffee at the sideboard and piling her plate high with an enormous breakfast.

For once Clarissa Worth also showed concern. "I'm sorry you've been feeling ill," she remarked. "I know how devastating a migraine can be." Her face brightened. "Freddie's roses are simply beautiful. Seth tells me he called upon you again last night, while we were at the Sanfords' party, and Seth gave him the message that you would play tennis this morning."

Abigail was dressed in a cotton skirt and middy blouse, her glossy black hair tied with a velvet ribbon. "Yes, I'm ready for a game. I feel ever so much better, thank you. Tell me, Father, how is My Clarissa? Are the workouts going along as smoothly as ever?"

Chauncey Worth beamed upon his daughter, thankful that she was apparently recovered from whatever had been bothering her. Women, he believed, like Thoroughbred horses, were prone to be temperamental and difficult to control. Therefore it was best, if possible, to overlook their vagaries.

"She is ready," he said proudly.

"My goodness," Clarissa remarked as she slit open an envelope with her silver letter knife, "do you two realize that the Season is practically over? There's the Travers on Saturday, the ball afterward at the United States, and that is about it."

"I, for one, am glad," Abigail said. "I'm growing weary of Saratoga, and I love New York in September."

Clarissa sighed. "It will be a busy winter. Mrs. Applegate informed me only yesterday that Hortense and Hal Staunton will announce their betrothal as soon as they return to the city, and that means endless prenuptial parties. Don't you think we should schedule a ball in their honor, Abigail?"

"Without question," her stepdaughter replied, determined to be cooperative. "Hortense has already asked me to be an attendant."

Mrs. Worth, delighted at the prospect of a whirlwind of activities, began to make rapid notes on a piece of paper. "It's not too soon to start planning," she remarked. "And hopefully, my dear, the announcement of your betrothal will follow soon thereafter."

Abigail did not reply, concentrating on her breakfast, for despite her heartbroken state, she discovered to her surprise that she was ravenous. Clarissa Worth, with a little sigh of disappointment, consoled herself with the realization that at least what had been bothering her stepdaughter lately seemed to be over and perhaps the excitement of the Travers stakes on Saturday and the Victory Ball would bring about what she had been longing for—Abigail's engagement to Freddie Freyhuysing.

That morning Abigail played a hard game of singles with Hal Staunton, followed by a doubles match with Freddie as her partner. It was as if by slamming the ball with her racquet instead of the gentle lobs that young ladies were expected to deliver, she could exorcise some of the misery that she had buried out of sight.

"You certainly made a fast recovery from your migraine, Abigail," Freddie exclaimed, wiping the perspiration from his face with a towel. Sally Winthrop, who was limp from fatigue, collapsed on a bench beside the court.

"We missed you last night, Abby," she said when she had finally caught her breath. "And you missed a particularly fascinating morsel of gossip."

Abigail laughed. "There is so much gossip floating around Saratoga, how can anyone keep up with it? But tell me, what is the latest?"

"Archibald Pomeroy has arrived at The Elms most unexpectedly. He attended the concert last night at the United States with his mother. My parents were there and talked with him, and my mother says he is the most attractive, dashing young man she has ever encountered. Too bad he has spent so much time in England, and none of us has had a chance to get acquainted."

Hal Staunton was smiling at Hortense. "Don't you dare fall for him, my girl," he said teasingly.

"But that's just the trouble," Sally continued lamentingly. "He's already betrothed to some titled English girl. I can't remember her name—Lady Something-or-other. That's undoubtedly why he lingered so long in London."

"Her name is Lady Ursula Huntington," Abigail burst out without thinking and could have bitten her tongue when she saw the startled expressions on all of their faces.

"And how did you know that?" Hortense asked. "Nobody knew he had arrived until last night."

"I was at tea at the Pomeroys the other afternoon. Long ago Mrs. Pomeroy and my mother were great friends, and she wanted to become better acquainted with me. While there, she mentioned her son was arriving from England and that he had become recently betrothed." Abigail was breathing more easily now, hopeful that her story would be accepted and very grateful when it apparently was.

"Fancy keeping such exciting news to yourself," Sally remarked before they launched into a discussion of the Travers stakes and how they all were wishing that My Clarissa would win.

Honoring her promise to herself to take each day in stride as if she didn't have a care in the world, Abigail accepted Freddie's invitation to join him in the promenade to Saratoga Lake.

She dressed with special care as if she were going to meet her lover and was rewarded by the adoration in Freddie's eyes as he helped her gingerly into his landau. She was wearing her blue crepe-de-chine gown that Mrs. Pomeroy had found so attractive when she went to The Elms the first time for tea, and today she carried a blue parasol that she opened with a graceful gesture as Freddie guided the vehicle along Broadway to join the long line of slowly moving carriages.

"You'll accompany me to the ball on Saturday night?" he asked shyly, and when she bowed her head in the affirmative, she could see that her acceptance had surrounded him in a delightful aura of bliss.

He's really a very decent person, she was thinking. He was certainly always immaculately turned out. Today he was wearing a white linen suit with a straw boater on his head, tilted at a rakish angle. Boaters had become the latest fashion for men in Saratoga since the Ivy League colleges had initiated shell racing on the lake.

They reached Moon's Lake House, which was situated on a hill overlooking the water. Freddie turned over the landau to a groom and they strolled down the hill. Finding a vacant bench they watched the passengers boarding the *Addie Smith* for a steamer ride to White Sulphur Spring.

"Want to go along?" Freddie asked.

She shook her head. "No, it's so peaceful right here, and it's fun to watch the sailboats on the lake. Freddie, why don't we buy a sailboat and come out every day next summer to take sailing lessons. I don't know the first thing about it, but it looks like great sport."

"You said—'we,' Abigail!" he said, stammering as he continued to gaze at the crowded pier with great concentration, watching the people laughing and jostling each other as they boarded the steamer.

"Yes—I said 'we,' Freddie," she said softly. "I think we could manage to get along very well together, don't you?"

She had not planned to commit herself this afternoon—the words had slipped out almost involuntarily—yet once spoken, she felt an immense relief that it had actually happened. How much of it was a desire to settle once and for all the question of her future and how much was a deep-seated need for revenge, to make Archibald Pomeroy aware that she was not nursing a broken heart, she was not able to determine.

He still did not glance in her direction. "But you don't love me, do you?" he finally asked.

"No, but I like and admire you very much."

"And it might become love. I've been told that often happens when two people marry." He turned to her eagerly. "Oh, Abby, won't you give it a try?"

"Yes, I'm willing if you are."

"If I am!" He grasped her hand in his, squeezing it until it hurt. "Abigail, surely you've known it's been my dearest wish for a very long time. You needn't even ask that question."

The steamer had departed, leaving a trail of foam in its wake. There were only a few visitors now strolling along the shaded paths.

"I wish we were alone, so I could kiss you," he said, blushing fiercely.

"Why don't you risk it?" she asked with an impish grin.

Their lips met and it was as she had known it would be—a sterile kiss that failed to arouse in her even the tiniest quiver of emotion.

"Mother will be very pleased," he mumbled, slipping an arm awkwardly across her shoulders.

Abigail laughed. "And so will Clarissa. She's been worried for some time for fear I'd become an old maid."

"You, an old maid—how ridiculous!" He pulled her close to him and she moved instinctively away. "I'm sorry, Abby," he murmured. "You'll have to watch out that I don't become carried away. It's difficult to be circumspect when I love you so much."

She opened her parasol and they strolled together up the slope to the hotel. Its tall white pillars were gleaming in the afternoon sun, the American flag on the cupola snapping in the breeze.

Over a glass of champagne on the piazza they sealed the bargain, as Abigail promised the betrothal would formally be announced upon her return to New York and solemnized in the early spring at the very latest.

"Must I wait so long for you?" Freddie asked.

"Yes," she said firmly. "For as I only intend to be married once, I want it to be perfectly programmed from the engagement party to the church wedding and finally the reception."

"Not to forget the honeymoon," he added and when she glimpsed an expression of delight mingled with triumph cross his face, she wondered if she would be able to go through with it after all. She felt great pity for Freddie sweep over her, and pity for herself, mixed with sorrow for what might have been if Archibald Pomeroy had only loved her.

Unwillingly her thoughts drifted back to

Kayaderosseras Creek, where Archibald Pomeroy had for the first time kissed her. What an electric moment that had been when she was introduced to the mysterious chemistry that can spring up without warning between a man and a woman.

To her it seemed strange that one kiss, one embrace, could have such a tremendous significance. With Freddie she knew the magic quality that existed between her and Archibald would never occur, and she couldn't help but wonder how Archibald and Lady Ursula Huntington responded when in each other's arms.

He had scoffed more than once at romantic love, making it very clear it was something he did not desire, something he had long since rejected. Now, regretfully, it was too late to attempt to prove to him that it was conceivable to fall in love and also find companionship and compatibility with your mate. All her instincts told her this was true.

She hadn't been listening to what Freddie was saying and when for the second time he described the engagement ring, a family heirloom his mother had promised to relinquish, she smiled and said, yes, she believed a cluster of diamonds and sapphires would be most appropriate.

At dinner that night Abigail dropped her surprise bombshell by stating quite casually, "By the way, I've decided to marry Freddie Freyhuysing."

At first Clarissa Worth was speechless but she finally recovered sufficiently to cry out breathlessly, "Abigail, how wonderful! When did this happen?"

"Today, at the Lake House. He's very much in love with me, and I grew tired of saying no."

Chauncey Worth gave her a thoughtful look. "I don't consider that a very good reason for becoming betrothed."

Abigail shrugged her shoulders with indifference. "At least I won't be hurt in the process, and, Father, although Freddie will never be the knight in shining armor that I used to foolishly think was waiting for me, he's really awfully decent and considerate. I believe we'll be as happy as most couples."

"What an exciting winter Season it will be," Clarissa exclaimed. "We'll have a formal engagement party and then the wedding itself—a church ceremony, naturally, with a huge reception afterward. I favor a candlelight service, don't you, Abigail?"

"Whatever you say, Clarissa," Abigail replied.

Clarissa, who had been puzzling over this unexpected announcement, attempting and failing to come up with a logical reason as to why her stepdaughter had accepted a suitor she obviously did not love, frowned and said with impatience, "You certainly don't sound ecstatic, but then I expect that's true of many prospective brides."

Abigail, deep in thought, did not answer. As her father suggested they open a bottle of champagne to celebrate the occasion, she rose obediently from the dinner table and followed him into the drawing room. But as they raised their glasses in a toast, she was not thinking of Freddie Freyhuysing but rather of a young man with red hair and hazel eyes, who had so skillfully captured her love only to reject it. Her silent toast was quite different from her father's, who said with a tender smile, "To Abigail and Freddie. May they find years of happiness together!"

No, her silent toast was quite different and would have horrified and displeased her father and stepmother. For as she raised her glass to her lips, she asked that somehow a miracle would occur and Archibald Pomeroy, discovering that it was she, not Lady Ursula Huntington who he truly loved, would come to her and ask for her hand in marriage.

Chapter Eighteen

On the day of the Travers an added air of excitement pervaded Saratoga. It could be felt on Broadway, at the springs, and on the piazzas of the famous hotels. The August Season was about to reach its climax.

Chauncey Worth was up before dawn to catch My Clarissa's final workout. His wife and daughter arose at a later hour, dressing leisurely in frocks that had been ordered from New York for the occasion—Clarissa in lilac, and Abigail in white with scarlet shoes and a matching parasol, a daring innovation started by Lillie Langtry.

They were driven to the track in the family victoria. Along the entire route vehicles of every description made their progress slow and tedious, and outside the entrance to the track they waited in a long line of carriages to disembark. It was another perfect August day. A morning fog had long since lifted, leaving the atmosphere crystal clear.

Clarissa and Abigail strolled to the walking ring

to watch the horses being led from the paddock by their trainers, while the jockeys, dressed in their owners' racing colors, awaited their arrival.

They lingered for a while by the walking ring, studying the horses with interest, and Abigail felt that My Clarissa outmatched them all in beauty and spirit. When it was drawing close to the time for the race to begin, they found their reserved seats in the grandstand, which was jammed with spectators.

A colorful panorama was spread out before their eyes: the sandy red track; the emerald-green infield; the brilliant-blue lake beside the tote board, with swans and ducks gliding across its still surface; and everywhere, on verandas and balconies, a profusion of petunias and geraniums.

Promptly at two o'clock an electric quality stilled the chatter of the crowd as the formal procession of horses, escorted by outriders in scarlet coats, appeared and as they drew near the starting gate a sudden hush fell over the racetrack.

To Abigail the suspense became almost unbearable, for she knew how much the race meant to her father. At first she was tempted to close her eyes until it was over, but soon she was on her feet, joining the rest of the spectators who were urging on their favorites as the horses thundered down the track.

A race which had meant months of work and preparation for the jockeys, the trainers, and the owners was over in a matter of minutes—with My Clarissa winning by half a length.

Proudly, with his wife and daughter, Chauncey Worth was escorted to the winner's circle, where My Clarissa stood, her glossy chestnut coat glistening in the bright sunlight, a thoroughly magnificent specimen—the winner of the oldest stakes race in the country. Her jockey was astride her, accepting congratulations, resplendent in the Worth racing colors of gold and blue.

After accepting the trophy, a silver plate, the presentation ceremony was over, and Chauncey Worth and his family were surrounded by well-wishers as the spectators spilled onto the track to catch a closer look at My Clarissa as she was led by her trainer back to the paddock, her moment of glory over.

Freddie was among the first to greet them and Abigail, completely caught up in the excitement, gave him an enthusiastic hug and burst out laughing when she saw that he was blushing.

As she moved through the crowd with her father and stepmother and Freddie by her side, she found herself face to face with Edwina Pomeroy and her son. She had been preparing herself for this event, sensing that sooner or later it might very well occur, but when she saw Archibald Pomeroy standing directly in front of her, close enough to touch, the proud defenses she had been building up over the past few days crumbled.

He was so handsome in his pearl-gray suit, his red hair blowing in the wind, his hazel eyes crinkling in a friendly smile, that he made every man around her become dull and insignificant. Mrs. Pomeroy stretched out her hand to congratulate Chauncey Worth and then introduced her son.

"Well," Chauncey said heartily, "I'm glad you managed to get to Saratoga in time for the Travers."

"I would have hated to miss it," Archibald said easily. "You must be very proud, Mr. Worth, of My Clarissa."

"I am, and it's high time we celebrate. Won't you join us for champagne?"

"Please do," Clarissa Worth exclaimed, and with her husband leading the way, they approached the stables. He led them to his favorite table on the veranda, where he often had breakfast during the morning work-out.

"What a shame," Clarissa was saying to Archibald, "that you have arrived at Saratoga at the end of the Season. You've missed some wonderful parties."

He was perfectly cool and composed as he pulled back a chair for his mother and seated himself beside her while Chauncey Worth ordered the champagne.

"I agree," he replied. "It's been far too brief a visit. We leave for New York on Monday and board our ship the following day. How much longer do you intend to stay in Saratoga?"

"Oh, there's so much to do before we go," Clarissa explained. "Closing up is such a bore. I don't suppose we'll be ready to leave until the end of next week."

Abigail Worth sat at the table between Freddie and her father, staring woodenly straight in front of her. As a waiter uncorked the champagne with a loud pop, and as they raised their glasses in a toast to My Clarissa, she studiously avoided Archibald's eyes.

Far too well brought up to ignore the amenities, however, she smiled across the table at Mrs. Pomeroy and asked if she were looking forward to an ocean voyage.

"I always find the sea air a tonic," Edwina Pomeroy replied. "And as Archie and I are fortunate enough to be excellent sailors, I expect the time will pass most pleasantly."

Clarissa was studying the son with a keen eye. What a marvelous catch he would have been for Abigail, she was thinking, regretful that a rumor was floating about regarding his betrothal to an English girl. But perhaps it was only a rumor, nothing more, she decided, and he will fall madly in love with Abigail overnight. Turning her gaze to her stepdaughter, she noted with approval that she had never presented a more stunning picture, although she was puzzled to see the girl had two bright spots of color on her cheeks and seemed to be going out of her way to ignore Mr. Pomeroy's presence.

"Abigail," she remarked in a slightly reproving tone, "perhaps you could introduce Mr. Pomeroy to some of your young friends. He might enjoy accompanying all of you to the Victory Ball."

"I have the notion," Abigail replied with icy calm, "that Mr. Pomeroy would find us far too young and immature. Am I correct in my assumption?" She was staring at Archibald and he stared back, an amused smile twisting his lips.

"I'm sure that wouldn't be the case," he answered in an even tone. "But unfortunately I must tender my regrets, for I've already promised to escort my mother to the ball."

"How very courtly of you." And turning to her father, Abigail said hurriedly, "Father, will you please excuse us? Freddie and I promised to meet some of our friends after the race."

"Certainly, my dear." Chauncey Worth scraped back his chair and stood up as she rose swiftly to her feet and grasped a slightly bewildered Freddie by the hand, making a hasty departure.

"Really, Abigail," Freddie murmured, "whatever got into you to leave so soon? It was quite rude, and I don't remember making any plans to meet our friends."

"Oh, hush, Freddie," she said crossly, and then just in case Archibald Pomeroy was watching their sudden exit, she tucked her arm in Freddie's and moved closer to him, whispering, "I wanted to be alone with you. Do you object?"

"Object, Abigail!" Freddie's face was aglow with pleasure and Abigail was assured that if Archibald were by any chance still observing them, they presented a perfect picture of an extremely happy, loving couple.

Clarissa Worth watched Abigail and Freddie disappear from view and, turning to the Pomeroys, she said in a mortified voice, "I apologize for my stepdaughter's behavior. I'm sure, Mr. Pomeroy, she didn't realize how abrupt she sounded. Young girls—" She shrugged her shoulders in a helpless gesture.

"No apologies necessary," he answered easily.

Chauncey Worth, springing to his daughter's defense, said testily, "Don't be tiresome, Clarissa. Abigail was merely attempting to give Mr. Pomeroy a graceful out if he desired it."

He returned to his favorite topic—My Clarissa—and his wife, sighing heavily, resigned herself to spending the next few days and possibly weeks reliving the Travers over and over again.

Chapter Nineteen

As Edwina Pomeroy sat in front of her dressing table mirror, making her final preparations for the Victory Ball at the United States, she wore a puzzled expression on her lovely face, which under soft lights still gave the illusion of youthfulness.

Priding herself on her gift of being able to analyze people's motives, particularly the members of her family, she continued to be confused as to why her son had decided to come out of hiding.

He had given her several reasons, none of which she considered entirely convincing. He had said he felt it was selfish of him not to exert himself a little and escort her to the closing festivities, which she could hardly attend alone. He had mentioned that he was temporarily unable to write, becoming stale due to too much concentration, and he had also confessed that, as he was lonely for the company of Lady Ursula Huntington, he believed a few activities might speed up the time until their departure.

But he had neglected to include Abigail Worth among his reasons, and at the track this afternoon, when they had come face to face with the Worths, she had not been fooled by his cool composure. In fact when Abigail had left the table so abruptly, barely tasting her glass of champagne, it had not escaped Mrs. Pomeroy's notice that her son's eyes as he followed her departure had contained a look bordering on despair.

All of this had led her to wonder if Archie were engaged in an inward struggle to forget the lovely young girl who had entered his life so dramatically. Perhaps his stubborn nature coupled with his extreme sense of loyalty prevented him from ending his alliance with Lady Ursula. Although she expected this might be the case, she was not completely certain, thereby hesitating to raise the subject of Abigail Worth again.

He was waiting for her in the entrance hall, resplendent in evening clothes, a striking young gentleman who stood out in a crowd no matter what he was wearing.

The doors had been flung open, their carriage was ready, and as Edwina Pomeroy stepped outside she noted that a full moon in a cloudless sky was bathing the driveway and the ancient elms in a muted, golden light.

"A romantic evening," she said to her son as he

assisted her into the landau and took over the reins.

As he agreed that it was, she detected all of the earmarks of lovesickness in his voice, but whether he was pining for Abigail or for Ursula was the question she was still unable to answer.

The United States Hotel was lit up brilliantly, and as their carriage approached, the strains of the orchestra drifted onto the piazza mingling with the voices and laughter of the assembled guests. She noted that Mrs. Horace Vandermark was seated in her usual prominent position with her son beside her, appearing thoroughly miserable and downcast. Observing the sad sight, Edwina was thankful that her own son, no matter how wrong he might be in his judgments, at least had a mind of his own.

They had promised to join the Chauncey Worth party, and as they entered the white marble lobby, she spotted them immediately, surrounded by exquisitely garbed ladies with their formally attired escorts.

"Where is your charming daughter?" she asked as she greeted her host.

"Oh, the young people have deserted us in favor of the garden," he said with a laugh. "Does it bring back memories, my dear Edwina, of our youth when we did the very same thing?" As he shook Archibald's hand Chauncey added, "Perhaps you would prefer to join them?"

Archibald shook his head firmly and, taking his mother's arm, guided her in the direction of the ballroom. After dancing with his mother he gallantly escorted Clarissa Worth to the floor.

"I understand," she said, giving him a penetrating look, "that you have become recently betrothed to an English girl. The rumor, if that's what it is, has caused a considerable stir in Saratoga."

"Her name is Lady Ursula Huntington," he replied evenly. "And I don't know why I continue to be amazed at how rapidly gossip travels about this town."

"It's probably because we don't have much else to occupy our minds," Clarissa replied with unusual candor. "Have you heard, by the way, that my stepdaughter is about to announce her betrothal too?"

It seemed to Clarissa that he lost a beat in the music as he almost stepped on her elegant satin slippers. Recovering from her fancy, she decided it was probably only in her imagination, as she could unearth no logical reason as to why he would be concerned about the future plans of Abigail.

"How splendid," he said as he whirled her about the floor. "Later I must seek her out to offer my congratulations."

It was close to midnight when Edwina Pomeroy became aware that Archibald was no longer seated at their table, and she found it difficult to follow the conversation around her as the possibility that he was seeking a rendezvous with Abigail Worth entered her mind.

Archibald had left only after a considerable amount of inward struggle, for since he had been convinced that sending the letter to Abigail was a sufficient apology, he did not consider that any further move on his part was necessary. No additional penance seemed required because of a few clandestine meetings, at which nothing of real significance had occurred. Surely, he argued, Abigail was far too intelligent to have taken any more seriously than he their mild flirtation, but if she had been hurt in the process, she had certainly bounced back with great rapidity by becoming immediately betrothed.

Nevertheless, while he talked with Chauncey Worth and danced with the various members of their party, he kept recalling Abigail's comments on Freddie Freyhuysing, which had been extremely devastating, wondering why, when she had recently felt that way, she had suddenly decided to marry him. Knowing firsthand how impulsive and unpredictable she could be, he became fearful that this was her method of revenge against him and that perhaps he had a responsibility to get to the bottom of the matter.

At last reaching the conclusion that he should talk to her at least once more, he had slipped away from the older people who were so deeply involved in reliving My Clarissa's stunning victory that they failed to take note of his departure.

Reaching the gardens, he stood in the shadows away from the dance floor and singled out Abigail immediately from the crowd. She was ravishing tonight in a misty-green gown, its full skirt scattered with rhinestones, her luxuriant black hair piled high on her head, crowned by a delicate tiara of diamonds. He had not realized before that she could be so proud and imperious. Up until this evening, he had always seen her with her glorious hair tumbling around her shoulders, but tonight she had become stately and dignified. She was more mature, no longer a harum-scarum girl to be teased and treated lightly, with the words she uttered dismissed as merely the thoughtless remarks of a young lady, still more child than woman.

The music ended and as she left the dance floor accompanied by a young man he had never seen before, he straightened his shoulders and walked up to her. Long before he reached her side she had seen him, and as he drew near, her cobalt-blue eyes were flashing with anger. As he bowed and said, "Good evening," she answered him cooly, introducing her partner as Harold Staunton.

Staunton returned his greeting and then made hurried apologies to leave, saying he must find his fiancée. For a brief time they stood on the edge of the dance floor in complete isolation.

"What made you decide to come out of hiding and honor us with your presence, Mr. Pomeroy?" she asked in a lofty manner. She was carrying a fan the same misty-green color as her dress, and as she fluttered it back and forth she avoided glancing in his direction, studying the people around them with great intensity.

"Abigail," he said in a low voice, "I want to apologize for pretending I was someone I was not. I didn't mean—" His voice trailed off as he realized she hadn't the least intention of forgiving him but was, in fact, thoroughly enjoying his discomfort.

"Don't give it another thought, Mr. Pomeroy," she continued airily. "As you said so succinctly in your beautifully constructed letter, there should be no regrets, and I couldn't agree with you more heartily."

"My first name happens to be Archibald," he replied with some heat. "As I believe we are friends, I should think you'd drop the 'Mr. Pomeroy.'"

"Oh, how foolish of me! You see, I believed all along it was Michael, and I must admit it's rather difficult for me to make the change."

"Abigail." He had reached the point of exasperation. "Will you at least look at me while we're talking?"

"Of course." She swung around and gave him a withering glance.

"Is it true you are betrothed to Freddie?" he asked.

"Yes." He saw a mixture of sorrow as well as anger in her eyes.

"And you love him? That's what I really want to know."

"Isn't one supposed to be in love when one decides to marry?" she retaliated. "Or is that too naive a question? But unlike you, when I make a decision of such serious nature, I announce it quite frankly to all my friends. I don't keep it undercover and flirt with one man when I'm promised to another."

"I gave you my apology," he said, his temper finally flaring.

"Which I accept!" With a graceful dip of her head she swept away and was immediately lost in the crowd.

He turned on his heel and left the garden. Finding his mother in the lobby, anxious to leave, he ordered their carriage to be brought to the front piazza of the hotel.

"Did you chat with Abigail Worth tonight?" his mother ventured, stealing a quick glance at his face, which was stern and remote.

"If you could call it a chat. I felt I owed her an apology—that my letter was not enough."

"How did she react?"

"She didn't seem to care one way or the other."

His mother sighed. "Women don't go around

wearing their hearts on their sleeves," she pointed out gently. "We, too, have our pride."

"She's betrothed to Freddie Freyhuysing, so I doubt very much if she's pining for me."

"Would you like her to pine for you?"

"No, how ridiculous! Yet somehow I'm adverse to her marrying this Freddie Freyhuysing. She's such a headstrong child. I dislike seeing her make a tragic mistake. Besides, he impresses me as such a spineless creature."

"She's not a child, Archibald," his mother pointed out. "She's eighteen and fully capable of making her own decisions. You wouldn't be coming down with a case of jealousy perhaps?"

"Certainly not!" His answer was explosive. "I've told you again and again, Mother, that I fully intend to marry Ursula, so why should I be jealous of what Abigail Worth decides to do? Sometimes I wish I had never come to Saratoga. Thank heavens we're leaving for England on Monday, for I yearn to get back to where everything will be the same—no unpleasant upheavals, just blessed peace and quiet."

They drove along in silence, reaching the outskirts of the village, where the road was bordered on either side by sweet-smelling pines. A cool breeze had sprung up carrying a promise of rain, and heavy clouds were beginning to obliterate the starlit sky. Edwina Pomeroy shivered and pulled her light cape more closely about her, wondering if she should tell this son of hers, who always appeared so certain of his decisions, that if he didn't know now, he would soon discover that nothing remains the same—ever.

Chapter Twenty

Abigail had always disliked seeing a house dismantled. The white sheets placed over the furniture seemed to her almost like shrouds, marking the end of so many experiences. In other years it had meant the end of simple pleasures—invigorating canters through the woods, early morning visits to the track, tennis matches, and the excitement of attending her first ball. But this year only sad memories prevailed—a hopeless love affair, tattered dreams, and promises that were born never to reach fruition.

As she watched the servants bustling about, intent with their dreary tasks, this year the house closing seemed to her to be especially poignant, for it meant the end of a familiar era and the beginning of a new life that failed to entrance her. Next August, when she returned to Saratoga, she would be married to Freddie. She would be living in his home, not here, and everything would be different.

Her announcement to her father and stepmother that she was betrothed to Freddie had miraculously changed the relationship between her and her stepmother. Clarissa Worth, immediately beginning to fill sheets of pristine white paper with detailed plans for the future, began to treat Abigail as a favorite sister rather than as a stepdaughter she considered fractious and tiresome.

But as far as her father was concerned, she sensed that he was not completely satisfied with her betrothal. Frequently she would catch him gazing at her with a troubled expression on his face, and she imagined he was recalling their early morning conversation at the track when she had confessed to him she was not one bit in love with Freddie Freyhuysing.

Her friends were all delighted by her announcement. None of them, with the exception of Hortense Applegate, had the slightest suspicion that she had accepted Freddie on the rebound.

At the outset Hortense had only vaguely sensed Abigail's unhappiness. It was not until their final day in Saratoga, when they were sitting in the gazebo, reminiscing about the events of the Season, that Hortense, who was noted for her directness, said bluntly, "Abigail, whatever is the matter? For a girl newly betrothed you are remarkably sad and pensive. Is it because you are not in love with Freddie and are already having second thoughts about marrying him?"

Abigail, finding herself desperately in need of unburdening herself to someone and knowing that Hortense could be trusted to keep her secret, spilled out the sad events that had led her down the road to an unhappy love affair.

Hortense did not interrupt her until she was completely finished and then she said angrily, "I think he treated you most shabbily, Abigail, and like it or not, you're well out of it."

To her great surprise, Abigail found herself heatedly defending Archibald Pomeroy. "It all started out in fun," she protested. "At the outset it was only a game. I'm convinced he never intended to hurt me."

"Did you really believe for one second that he was a farm boy?"

"Yes and no." Abigail was discovering it was a great relief to be able to analyze her feelings openly with a sympathetic friend. "He never dressed like a gentleman but on the other hand he spoke and acted like one. For a while I believed he might be Archibald Pomeroy, until his mother stated flatly that he had remained in London. When I couldn't imagine who else it might be, I became half convinced that he really was Michael Sullivan, who by reading and studying on his own, had acquired an excellent vocabulary and a certain amount of polish."

"But he was cowardly enough to end the entire affair with a letter!" Hortense spoke scornfully.

"Yet he did apologize at the Victory Ball," Abigail said, springing once more to his defense. "Of course, I ruined it all by being haughty and disdainful."

"I'm glad you were—it was precisely what he deserved."

Abigail smiled ruefully. "I'm not glad now. I'm sorry. It was my beastly pride getting in the way. If only I had been gracious and forgiving, we might at least have had a dance together and parted on a more amicable note. I keep thinking maybe, just maybe, he would have found me irresistible."

"What is one dance!" Hortense pointed out. "It would probably only have served to make you more distraught, knowing all the time that he was betrothed to another girl."

"I suppose so. I keep wondering and wondering what she is like."

"She must be very beautiful. She would have to be if he prefers her over you."

"If I had met him first, maybe it would have turned out differently," Abigail said mournfully, her eyes filling with tears.

Hortense shook her head impatiently. "But it didn't happen that way, Abigail," she said with firmness. "And you'll merely make yourself more miserable if you insist on reliving it over and over again, saying maybe this, maybe that would have changed the situation." She hesitated a moment before asking uneasily, "What do you intend to do about Freddie?"

Abigail looked up at her in surprise. "Why, marry him, naturally. I've already promised him that I would."

"How can you when you're in love with another man?"

"I'll manage." Abigail spoke grimly. "No one will ever suspect how I feel but you."

"Freddie will know. Are you being fair to him?"

"I told him at the time we became betrothed that I was not in love with him, and he was willing to go ahead and take the gamble."

"Well, I suppose that's fair enough," Hortense replied, and then she added softly, "Poor Freddie!"

They sat in the gazebo for a while longer, Hortense saddened that her dearest friend was experiencing so much grief, Abigail relieved to have at last been able to share her sorrow. Later when they strolled through the garden toward the main house, Abigail, for the first time, noticed that the leaves on the maple trees on the side lawn were beginning to turn to flame, marking the end of the Saratoga Season. With a proud toss of her head, she pledged that tomorrow when they returned to

New York she would begin to forget Archibald Pomeroy and all the might-have-beens. She would concentrate singlemindedly on building a satisfactory life with Freddie Freyhuysing.

Chapter Twenty-one

Believing that action might serve as a panacea for a broken heart, upon her return to New York Abigail threw herself into a frenzied round of activities.

The formal announcement of her betrothal to Freddie Freyhuysing was scheduled for October with an afternoon reception at the Worth Fifth Avenue mansion. Clarissa had urged that the wedding take place immediately after the Christmas holidays, but Chauncey Worth, vaguely perceiving that his daughter was going through some kind of difficult adjustment, surprised his wife by remaining adamant to her suggestion, saying firmly, "It will be sometime in the spring, for that is when Abigail seems to desire it and, after all, she will be the bride."

Clarissa, eventually accepting defeat, became so embroiled in the complicated details of planning a betrothal party and a wedding, that days would go by before she would complain to her husband that he was neglecting her in New York as he had in Saratoga, spending far too much time at his clubs. With such an unexpected reprieve, Chauncey Worth began to wish that he had several other marriageable daughters waiting in the wings.

It was not difficult for Abigail to become involved in a busy daily program. A ride in Central Park on Matilda in the early morning, luncheon with some friends, tedious afternoon teas, and countless dinner parties and balls filled up her days and weeks, and with Hortense Applegate's wedding set for November, the number of social events snowballed until she found it difficult to concentrate on what to wear to the next event. Soon it became necessary to replenish her already extensive wardrobe.

For once she was grateful for these distractions, and as the invitations in thick white envelopes accumulated, she discovered that each day her thoughts returned to Saratoga and Archibald Pomeroy with less and less frequency.

She also learned that being betrothed to Freddie had its compensations. It meant that her stepmother ceased warning her that she was in danger of becoming an old maid, and as long as Abigail agreed more or less enthusiastically with Clarissa's nuptial plans, tranquillity descended upon their household.

There was only one upheaval to mar the placid

days. She mentioned that she was enrolling in a course on the history of art, being offered by the Metropolitan Museum. Inheriting from her mother an interest in paintings, she found herself eager to learn more on the subject.

Clarissa Worth had objected strongly, stating that there simply wasn't enough time to waste on dreary lectures. Her father hemmed and hawed, not certain whose side to take, when much to her gratitude Freddie intervened and came to the rescue, saying he highly approved of the idea, and thereby tipped the scales in her favor.

She considered her relationship with Freddie a pleasant one, and although her heart never missed a beat when he kissed her, she began to believe that her present state of mind was preferable to August in Saratoga, when the ups and downs caused by her clandestine meetings with Archibald Pomeroy had brought her to the edge of despair.

She even went so far as to convince herself that to marry a man you liked but did not love was far more sensible than risking the pitfalls of a tempestuous love affair, comparing her present position to safely drifting in a boat on the placid waters of a pond as against venturing down the dangerous rapids of a turbulent stream that threatened at any moment to capsize your craft.

In October the announcement party was held

with even the critical Clarissa declaring it a great success. Abigail, dressed in a rose velvet gown, had never appeared more strikingly lovely. She and Freddie stood beside their parents in the vast hallway of the Worth's town house, greeting the guests while a string quartet, screened from view behind graceful ferns, played the most popular melodies of the day.

There was an elaborate tea served in the drawing room for the older people, an orchestra in the ballroom for the younger set. Champagne was served to toast the future happiness of Abigail and her fiancé. As the afternoon wore on and all of the guests had been properly greeted, Chauncey Worth and his compatriots retired to the library to enjoy drinks of sterner stuff and to reminisce over past races at Saratoga and their luck or lack of luck at cards the night before.

"Are you happy, Abigail?" Freddie asked.

They were dancing their first dance together as a betrothed couple, and she detected a note of anxiety in his voice. *Poor Freddie*, she thought, for despite the fact she was now wearing the magnificent diamond and sapphire engagement ring he had given her, he still did not believe she had really accepted him—that the elusive Abigail Worth, who had held him at a distance for such a long time and who had always been close by but still out of reach, had finally consented to become his wife.

Smiling at him gently she said, "Yes, Freddie, I am." If finding a peaceful harbor to anchor in away from storms and tidal waves meant happiness, well then she was telling him the truth.

In November Hortense was married. It was a splendid affair, with Hortense, stately and beautiful in white satin, sweeping down the church aisle on her father's arm.

Selected as her maid of honor, Abigail stood by the altar. As she listened to the familiar words of the wedding service and the clear, ringing responses of Harold Staunton and his bride, she experienced an onrush of panic when it was brought home to her that in very few months she would be standing in the exact spot where Hortense stood today. Mrs. Frederick Freyhuysing! She had never cared for the name. What if she found herself unable to go through with the ceremony? Closing her eyes, she had an all too vivid picture of picking up her voluminous skirts and racing down the aisle past her beautifully gowned stepmother, who wore a look of utter horror on her face. She shook her head dazedly and began to concentrate once more on the exchange of vows. The ceremony over, the organ began the stirring recessional and being brought back abruptly to the present, Abigail bent down to straighten Hortense's magnificent lace train as she turned from the altar, smiling tremendously at her husband.

Abigail walked beside Freddie down the aisle behind the newly married couple and all the way fought valiantly to hold back her tears. On the steps of the church as they waited for their carriage, Freddie slipped his arm tenderly around her shoulders. "I know, darling," he whispered, "exactly what you were thinking. Soon it will be you and I standing there. I can hardly wait."

Impatiently she brushed the tears from her cheeks, thinking what a blessing it was that people were unable to read the minds of others, and that her dear, reliable fiancé hadn't the slightest inkling of the horrible nightmare she had just experienced in the church.

Chapter Twenty-two

It was on a gray morning in December, the sky heavy with leaden clouds, the first snowstorm of the season predicted, when Chauncey Worth, seated at the breakfast table, ruffled the waters of Abigail's hard-won, tranquil existence.

"This is certainly the year for betrothals," he remarked. "Young Archibald Pomeroy is marrying some English girl. Too bad—somehow I always like to see Americans marry Americans."

Clarissa wrinkled her nose in disapproval of his last remark. "Don't be plebeian, darling," she said.

Chauncey began to laugh, thoroughly amused by his wife's occasional malapropisms and knowing that if he were tactless enough to compare his wife's antecedents to his, she would come out a very poor second.

"When will they be married?" Abigail asked, disturbed by her violent reaction to her father's casual announcement, afraid to take her eyes off her plate for fear she would reveal the sudden panic that without warning had possessed her.

"Not until sometime in February. But they're coming to New York for Christmas. That means the Pomeroy place will be opened. I thought I saw a great deal of activity around there the other day when I drove by."

"I wonder what she's like?" Clarissa pondered. "He is such an extremely handsome fellow. It's unfortunate, Abigail, you never had the opportunity to get to know him."

When Abigail did not reply, her stepmother sighed and returned to the morning's mail. "I wonder if they'll give a party," she mused. "I've always wanted to see the inside of that house." The Pomeroy mansion was frequently compared to J. P. Morgan's tremendous pile and for some time it had annoyed Clarissa to see such a splendid building unoccupied.

"I believe they'll have a ball," Abigail said. "Mrs. Pomeroy told me the day I had tea with her that the next time they journeyed to New York she planned to entertain."

"How marvelous," Clarissa exclaimed. "You know, I'm not sure which I'm more curious to see, the house or Archibald's fiancée."

"What is possibly of more importance," Chauncey intervened dryly, "is that I learned at the club recently that this Pomeroy fellow has written a novel which apparently is expected to create quite a few waves in England and over here when it appears."

"You aren't telling me, Chauncey," Clarissa asked with some sarcasm, "that they discuss more serious matters than gambling and racing at your club?"

"But, of course I am, my dear," he replied, successfully concealing his irritation at her barbed question. "We become involved in all sorts of serious subjects and this chap's book exploring the social ills of England during the reign of Victoria is to be published within the next few months."

Abigail, unable to listen to one more word on the subject of the Pomeroys, rose abruptly from the table.

"What are your plans for today?" her stepmother asked.

"My class at the museum this morning," Abigail replied, "and a series of at homes in the afternoon."

"Oh, your stuffy old class," Clarissa said impatiently, "which reminds me, Chauncey, the director of the Metropolitan called here the other day. He's having an exhibition of Sargent portraits during the holiday season and wants to add ours to the collection. I said no, naturally."

Chauncey raised his eyes from the sporting pages. "Get in touch with him and tell him we've changed our minds," he replied tersely.

"Whatever for?" Clarissa said angrily. She had been vastly irritated when her husband, upon their return from Saratoga, had refused to remove his first wife's portrait from the drawing room, and now here he was placing her in an even more untenable position by allowing it to go on public display, causing the inevitable comparison between the first and second Mrs. Worths, which would certainly put her at a disadvantage.

"Because," said Chauncey, "it is one of his best and an exhibit without it would not be complete."

Clarissa, overwhelmed by the steely quality in his reply, controlled her temper and said to Abigail as she made her departure, "Will you tell the director when you see him that I've changed my mind?"

The Pomeroys arrival in New York caused a considerable sensation among the very rich, and when invitations were mailed by them to attend a ball at their Fifth Avenue mansion the day after Christmas, the afternoon teas and evening dinner parties buzzed with rumors as to who had been invited and who had not.

To Abigail's dismay not only had her father and stepmother been included but so had she and Freddie. As it had by now been rated the biggest event of the holidays, there was not the slightest chance of refusing. Besides, as the day drew near, she found herself, like Clarissa, curious to meet Archibald's fiancée.

She spent a long time debating what to wear for the occasion, finally settling for a gown of ivory velvet. Freddie had presented her with a sapphire necklace for Christmas and with her diamond tiara crowning her luxuriant black hair, she knew when she took a final look in her mirror that it was highly unlikely Lady Ursula Huntington would outdistance her tonight, at least as far as appearances were concerned.

The entrance hall, where the Pomeroys greeted their guests, was exquisitely decorated with huge wreaths of laurel and holly and copper tubs of scarlet poinsettias. An evergreen, reaching two stories high, stood in the center of the marble floor, its branches aglow with hundreds of tiny candles.

Abigail, standing beside her fiancé in the receiving line among a group of friends, wore a bright, fixed smile on her lovely face, unable to absorb one word of the conversation that was swirling around her. As they drew near to their hosts she was, without warning, seized by an almost overpowering desire to turn and run away out into the cold, black night. With a great effort she managed to control her panic and when she approached Mrs. Pomeroy, she stretched out her hand and smiled, outwardly appearing calm and self-possessed.

"My dear Abigail," Edwina Pomeroy cried out

warmly, kissing her on the cheek before introducing her to the ambassador. Abigail drew in her breath sharply as she offered him her white-gloved hand, for he was an older edition of his son, his red hair streaked with silver, his gray eyes warm and thoughtful.

Her meeting with Archibald turned out to be something of an anticlimax, over almost before it had begun. Stiff smiles were exchanged, cool handshakes given before he presented his fiancée, who acknowledged the introductions abstractedly as if she had grown completely bored by the whole proceeding.

Afterward as they moved up the circular staircase to the ballroom, Freddie whispered in her ear, "Lady Ursula reminds me of one of your father's horses, but I can't recall at the moment which one."

"Freddie," Abigail exclaimed reprovingly, "it's not like you to make such a scathing remark!" But despite herself she found herself laughing with him, for she had had the identical reaction. "She's probably a very fine person," she continued. "In fact I've been told she is noted for her sterling character."

"Sterling it may be," Freddie replied, "but along with it she's as cold and formidable as an iceberg, and I fervently hope our acquaintanceship never progresses beyond a formal handshake. I wonder if that Pomeroy fellow realized what he was missing, Abigail, when he greeted a warm and loveable girl like you as he stood beside his frosty fiancée?"

Tempted to tell him that Archibald Pomeroy was not enamored by warm and loveable girls, preferring the erudite, intellectual type, she stopped her remark just in time and instead gave Freddie's hand a squeeze. She was pleased by his compliment and happy that their relationship had progressed to a point where she found herself suffering his company, discovering unexpected qualities under his shy exterior that she was growing to admire. *I could have done lots worse,* she told herself as she and Freddie stood on the edge of the dance floor while her program was swiftly filled by a ring of admirers.

Relieved that her meeting with Archibald Pomeroy had not been as painful an experience as she had imagined, nevertheless as the evening progressed Abigail found herself constantly searching the crowded room for a glimpse of him, and although the orchestra was superb and her partners excellent dancers, for her the ball disintegrated merely into something to get through as quickly as possible.

Freddie, sharing a waltz with her, noticed her extreme pallor with concern. "Is something wrong, Abigail?" he asked anxiously. "Do you want to leave?"

She shook her head, firmly determined to stay until the very last note of music was played, to prove to Archibald Pomeroy, if he cared at all to know, that she was managing her life superbly without him and was completely undisturbed at being a guest in his house.

At midnight an elaborate buffet was served and afterward the dancing continued in the ballroom. It was growing late, the crowd was thinning out, and Freddie was remarking that perhaps it was time to leave, when she heard the only voice in the world that had the power to set her senses tingling. Archibald Pomeroy was asking her to dance, and before she could refuse, she was in his arms and he was spinning her lightly across the floor.

"You could hardly turn me down at my own party," he said with his engaging grin. As their eyes met she knew that nothing had changed, that it would never change, and she would always be desperately in love with him.

All too soon the dance ended. Freddie was waiting for her at the entrance to the ballroom, and holding her head proudly erect, she smiled and said a casual "Good night."

But as she turned to leave him, he grasped her hand, pulling her close as he said, the urgency in his voice unmistakable, "Am I still not forgiven?"

She gave him a scornful glance, answering him

coldly. "If your conscience is bothering you, Archibald, forget it. What happened this summer in Saratoga has become inconsequential, so you see, there is nothing to forgive."

The weary musicians were packing up their instruments. They were alone on the dance floor, completely oblivious to the fact that Freddie was approaching them, a worried expression on his face. Still they did not move away from each other but continued to stand in the center of the room, hands clasped, immobile, and as Abigail's eyes told him that the words she had spoken were empty and meaningless, his eyes told her that he too had not forgotten last summer in Saratoga.

Spellbound, she knew that he was spellbound too. It was Freddie's voice, mild and gently reproving, that at last drew them back to reality. As if in a dream they parted, he thanking her formally for the dance, she simply saying good night.

It was time to leave. She moved in a trance toward the large room on the third floor, adjacent to the ballroom, where the ladies cloaks had been hung. A maid handed her the floor-length ermine cape her father had given her for Christmas, but before putting it on, she crossed to one of the dressing tables and studied her face in the gilt-edged mirror.

It was flushed and her cobalt-blue eyes seemed

to be twice their normal size. She was breathing heavily and, struggling to regain a measure of composure, she closed her eyes and was back in his arms again.

Throughout the evening she had yearned for one dance with him, and at last it had taken place. Now, because of this, she knew, without a doubt, that it was not and never had been a question of unrequited love.

He loved her too! His love was so unmistakably clear that it had not been necessary to exchange one word. *I belong to him and he to me,* she told her reflection in the mirror. *How tragic that we have allowed ourselves to become enmeshed in an untenable situation from which there is no way to be extricated. He is betrothed to Lady Ursula and I to Freddie, and it is far too late to change, to admit our love to each other and to the world.*

Turning from the mirror, she shivered and, pulling her cape closely about her, left the dressing room and found Freddie waiting outside to escort her to their carriage.

"Are you all right, Abigail?" Freddie asked. "Too much dancing perhaps?"

"Yes, too much dancing," she replied.

In the carriage driving homeward she was silent, resting her head against the soft cushions, her eyes closed.

Reaching home, he slipped his arms about her shoulders and kissed her. Listlessly she responded, her lips cold and unresponsive and as she did, she wondered how she had ever believed for one moment that she could attain happiness with Freddie Freyhuysing.

Chapter Twenty-three

Edwina Pomeroy had been eagerly looking forward to her visit to New York, anxious to return to familiar haunts and renew old friendships. But a good measure of her high spirits diminished as she found herself, on a day-to-day basis, in the company of Lady Ursula Huntington.

At the outset Lady Ursula had made it clear that she did not want to accompany them, preferring to remain in England until Mrs. Pomeroy had pointed out that as she was marrying her son, it behooved her to be gracious and meet their many relatives and friends in America.

From the very beginning of the journey, the two women had not experienced a comfortable relationship, and by the time they reached the Fifth Avenue mansion, Edwina Pomeroy was utterly exasperated with her future daughter-in-law, by this time wishing heartily she had never insisted Lady Ursula accompany them.

To compound an already complicated situation,

she often caught her son off-guard, glancing at Lady Ursula with a far from loving expression, convincing her that Archibald realized Ursula was not turning out to be the perfect companion he had visualized and that it was only his stubbornness and pride that prevented him from dissolving the betrothal.

The night of their ball she had felt a tug of regret as she greeted Abigail Worth in the receiving line, finding her even more beautiful than she had remembered. Later in the evening when she observed Archibald and Abigail dancing together, perfectly complementing each other, it had taken every ounce of restraint on her part not to confront her son after the last guests had departed to accuse him of blindness and stupidity as far as affairs of the heart were concerned.

As the time drew near for their departure to England and she saw the rapidly increasing strained relationship between Archibald and Ursula, she felt a vague stirring of hopefulness that a break between them might occur before it was too late. The wedding had been scheduled for early February, soon after their return to London, and she knew it would be almost unbearable for her to be forced to witness the event.

On New Year's Day Archibald left the house alone—to where she did not know. Lady Ursula sequestered herself in her room to write letters and

Edwina Pomeroy sought out her husband in the library, finding the need to unburden her anxieties.

"Archibald, can't you talk to your son?" she demanded.

"What about, my dear?" he asked mildly, fully aware of why his wife was upset but determined, in his own mind, that it was his son's problem, not theirs, and that they would be foolish to interfere.

"I just can't bear to see Archie so miserable," she cried out. "The reason why is obvious to me if not to you. He's not in love with Ursula, not in the least, but he is too pig-headed, refusing to admit he has made a dreadful mistake."

"Edwina, dear, sit down," her husband said quietly. "Let's talk this over sanely and sensibly. You must remember that Archie is a man and no matter how strongly you object to this marriage, you have no right to tell him so. In fact I feel it would be a futile gesture and might only serve to harden his resistance."

"You mean we should sit idly by and see this marriage take place?"

"I'm afraid we have no other choice."

"Even if it means years of unhappiness for him?"

"Yes, he must make his own decision."

Edwina sighed. "If only I could bring myself to even like Ursula, but I can't. I've found it quite impossible to do so. Since arriving here she has complained constantly about almost everything—the noise and confusion on our streets, the extremely cold weather. She's stiff and aloof with all of our friends, and she seems to delight in conveying the impression that she can barely tolerate her sojourn in the Colonies."

Archibald Pomeroy laughed. "Ah, yes, I believe she belongs with a goodly number of the British who still refuse to concede that they lost the Revolution."

"To make matters worse," Edwina continued, "I'm almost certain Archie is in love with someone else."

"You are? Who?" Her husband glanced at her curiously.

"A girl named Abigail Worth."

"Abigail Worth," he repeated. "Ah, yes, I remember meeting her the night of our ball. She's a charming young lady, as beautiful as her mother."

"I'm extremely fond of her. They met in Saratoga during the Season. I'm certain she loves him too."

"Isn't she also betrothed?"

"Unfortunately—yes."

"What a tangle," her husband exclaimed. "But, Edwina, it is not up to us to untangle it. I forbid you to attempt to do so. It's Archie's problem and if he makes a wrong judgment, he must live with it. Promise me, my darling, you won't say one word to him about this?"

Edwina Pomeroy spread out her hands in a helpless gesture. "All right, I promise," she said reluctantly. "But what a dreadful price Archie is about to pay if he has to spend the rest of his life with Lady Ursula."

"I think we should take a ride in the carriage," Archibald Pomeroy said briskly. "It's a cold, bright day and it will blow the cobwebs out of our brains."

That was the end of Edwina Pomeroy's attempt to persuade her husband to intervene in her son's dilemma. But when she attended the balls and receptions which took place their last few days in America, it was with a heavy heart and without much hope that her son would throw his cap to the winds and decide that life without Abigail Worth would be an extremely dull and dismal journey.

Reluctantly she concluded that the entire situation had deteriorated to a point of no return: her son committed to Lady Ursula, Abigail committed to Freddie, with time running out on them both. *If only*, she thought despairingly as she and her husband drove through Central Park, bundled in fur rugs because of the cold, *if only there was some way I could arrange for them to be thrown together.*

Her husband, who knew her so well, must have guessed her thoughts, for he gave her a warning glance and said, "Remember your promise, Edwina!"

"I'll remember," she replied. "But, Archibald, mark my words, someday you and I will both regret that we lacked the courage to intervene."

Chapter Twenty-four

As the holiday season drew to a close, one gala affair followed swiftly on the heels of another, and although Abigail and Archibald attended many of the same functions, they were studiously careful to avoid another direct confrontation. Often they danced past each other—they never danced together. It was as if they had made an unspoken pledge that to find themselves in each others arms again could only lead to disaster.

Somehow, someway, Abigail managed to hide her misery from her father and stepmother and, most important of all, from Freddie. I'm very fond of him, she kept telling herself over and over again, as if repeating the sentence like a litany would make everything turn out all right in the end.

It was true that she had grown fond of Freddie, considering him a thoroughly nice though innocuous young man, but unfortunately for Abigail she had also discovered that being fond of someone was not enough and that once love awakened you, all other men but one became pallid and insignificant.

So as the days sped by she knew that the only hope of a reprieve was to manage to exist until the hour that the Pomeroys closed their town house and left for England, believing their departure might give her at least a slender chance to forget this man who had so easily made her his prisoner. New Year's Eve came and she and Freddie, returning late from a party, exchanged a final toast before bidding each other good night, with Freddie remarking triumphantly, "Now, Abigail, I can say we are to be married this year—1895, and I promise you, my darling, it will be the most spectacular year of our lives."

If he noticed that her smile was sad, he said nothing, adding, "All that remains is for you to set the date. Which month do you prefer, April or May? And what do you think of spending our honeymoon in Europe?"

"Europe would be fine," Abigail replied listlessly, and seeing the expression of dogged devotion in his eyes, she gave him a hurried kiss as she escorted him to the door.

On New Year's Day, the men, as was their custom, repaired to their clubs and Freddie, who had recently become a proud member of the Union League, had asked Abigail almost timorously if she would mind if he did not call upon her until the evening. With a laugh she assured him it was all right, ashamed to discover that it would be a welcome relief to be free of him, if only for a few hours, when she could abandon any attempt at pretense and subterfuge and try to sort out her muddled emotions.

New Year's Day dawned crisp and clear with only a light powder of sparkling snow on the ground. Elated to be free at last from any engagements, Abigail collected her skates, ordered a carriage, and driving to Central Park felt her spirits lifting.

It was such a marvelous day that as she skated around the rink the gaiety and excitement all about her became contagious and for the first time since the Pomeroys' ball she became exhilarated and almost lighthearted.

She was wearing a tartan wool skirt, and a short mink jacket with matching muff and hat completed the smart outfit. The wind whipped her cheeks until they were pink. A band was playing a martial tune and, as she skated faster and faster, keeping time to the beat of the music, she was thinking how wonderful it was to be alone and unfettered—if only for a brief hour or so, to forget about Freddie and their wedding in the spring, and yes, even to forget Archibald Pomeroy and the impossible situation which had developed between them.

A skater swept by, jogging her elbow, and losing her balance, she hit a crack in the ice and fell with a crash. Feeling a sharp twinge in one ankle, she gave a cry of pain and closed her eyes for a second. When she opened them she was surrounded by a swarm of people. Someone was cradling her in his arms and, gazing upward, she discovered to her amazement that her rescuer was Archibald.

"What are you doing here?" she cried out, instinctively drawing away from him.

"Anyone can come to Central Park," he replied easily. "The important question is, are you all right?"

"I think so—I believe I cracked my head a bit on the ice and my ankle hurts, but I'll survive."

"Do you think you can stand up?" he asked and with his help she pulled herself to her feet. "Are you sure you're not hurt?" he asked again.

Gingerly she tested her ankle. "It's obviously not broken or sprained. I'm fine—I only lost my dignity."

She was glad to see they had lost their concerned audience, for the crowd, deciding that she was not seriously injured and was well taken care of, had dissolved. Holding her arm, he guided her to a bench at the edge of the rink.

"I didn't know you could skate," he said.

"There are a lot of things you don't know about me."

"Where's Freddie?"

"At his club. And Ursula?"

"She doesn't enjoy the cold weather."

They were both staring straight ahead, reluctant, afraid to look at each other.

"I don't suppose you're up to trying it again?" he finally asked.

"I think I'd better. We'll soon freeze to death, sitting on this cold bench."

He rose and pulled her to her feet. It was a glorious sensation to be gliding across the ice together, hands crossed, with the band playing a sprightly melody. People sped past them. A little boy struggled by, his ankles flopping. As he stumbled and fell, Archibald bent down and scooped him up, brushing the snow off his jacket. After a while, breathless and laughing, they found another bench and collapsed on it.

"Do you know what I want more than anything else in the world?" she asked, her eyes dancing. "I want one of those wonderful mugs of hot chocolate they serve in the park restaurant, topped with layers upon layers of whipped cream."

He left to retrieve their boots and when he returned they sat on the bench, unlacing their skates. Abigail's hands had become red and stiff from the cold and without a word he rubbed them vigorously until they were warm again. They found a table in the restaurant and ordered.

She sipped her chocolate thoughtfully and with a spoon began to tackle the whipped cream.

"There's nothing more delectable than hot chocolate on a wintry afternoon."

He grinned and, taking his napkin, carefully wiped the corners of her mouth. "You're delectable," he told her. "Even with whipped cream smeared all over your face."

She found the little homely gesture almost more than she could bear.

His face became serious once more. "Abigail," he said, his voice low and tense, "we can't go on like this."

"I know." She concentrated fiercely on her hot chocolate.

"What are we going to do?"

"What can we do? We're both betrothed. We'll have to marry, I suppose, and make the best of it." At last she looked up at him, managing a weak smile, but he saw that her eyes were swimming with tears. "In time we'll forget."

"I doubt that. What a fool I've been." He ran his hand through his thick, wiry hair until it was standing on end and tenderly she stretched out her hand and smoothed it back in place.

"You see, Abigail," he went on distractedly, "I'm a very stubborn fellow. I made up my mind long ago that I would avoid frivolous debutantes like the plague. When you came into my life so unexpectedly—" he broke off, laughing as he recalled his first meeting with her when she came out of the thicket in her ridiculous costume.

"Well," he continued, "when I met you I was already engaged to Ursula, so I convinced myself you were what I didn't want. You were far too beautiful, too young, too immature. That's what I told myself. I feared that you would lead me a merry chase. My mother was wiser than I, so much wiser. She knew better. She tried to tell me more than once that I was wrong, but I wouldn't listen."

"Well, I was equally at fault," Abigail said soberly. "After I received that letter from you, I became betrothed to Freddie out of sheer spite and false pride. I wouldn't even accept your apology that night at the Victory Ball."

"We've certainly made a hash of things," he replied. They finished their hot chocolate and sat at the table in utter misery, their high spirits when they had glided around the rink completely dashed.

"What are we going to do?" he repeated in desperation.

"What can we possibly do at this late date to change things? It's progressed too far for either of us not to honor our promises. I've become very fond of Freddie. He truly loves me. I couldn't—I simply couldn't bear to hurt him, to disgrace him in front of all his friends."

"I couldn't do that to Ursula either."

"When do you leave for England?" she asked.

"In three days."

"Archibald," she said and bending across the table she touched his cheek gently, "I love you—I always have from the first moment we met. But it wasn't until recently—that night at your parents' ball—that I knew with certainty you returned my love. I guess the knowledge of that will have to console me in the months and years ahead. How sad it is that it took so long for us to discover what we meant to each other."

She stood up, collecting her skates and her muff. "It's time to go, but we must pledge never to meet again. That is the only solution, the only way we will be able to survive."

He slowly nodded his head in agreement, paid for the hot chocolate, and followed her out of the restaurant and into the park.

"Will you hail a carriage for me?" she asked in a small voice.

Without a word he did.

"Good-bye, Archibald," she said and when he attempted to kiss her, she moved away from him and climbed into the carriage, giving the driver her address.

As they pulled away from the curb she did not look back. It was impossible for her to look back. The new-found knowledge that he loved her, instead of bringing her great joy, merely served to make her sorrow even more difficult to bear.

Chapter Twenty-five

There were no parties scheduled for New Year's night. After dinner Freddie called on Abigail and they spent the evening playing a desultory game of chess in the library.

He was surprised when he won the first two games with ease, for he had discovered that Abigail was an excellent player and more often than not the winner.

"You're not concentrating, darling," he said, gently reproving her. "Or have you decided to be generous tonight?"

"No, you've won fairly and squarely, Freddie," she assured him. "But I've had enough chess for tonight and so I imagine have you. I'm tired from all the holiday festivities. For once let's make it an early evening."

He agreed and she walked with him to the front door, but when he put his arms about her to kiss her farewell, she closed her eyes and tried not to appear as if she were doing penance.

Suffering his kiss, she opened her eyes and saw that he was staring at her with an expression of deep sorrow. "I wonder if you will ever love me, Abby?" he asked.

Mustering a smile, she answered, "Of course I will, but you must be patient with me, Freddie, and give me more time. You know that I've become very fond of you."

"Very fond of me," he repeated, shrugging into his heavy winter overcoat. "I guess for now I'll have to be content with that."

After he had gone she wandered back to the library, opened a book, tossed it aside and, curling up in a deep sofa by the hearth, stared at the leaping flames without seeing them. She was again at Kayaderosseras Creek with Archibald Pomeroy and he was holding on to Matilda's reins, reaching up to kiss her, and she knew the perfection of that episode would never be forgotten.

She thought as she had often thought before: What if she had allowed him to pull her down from her horse? What if she had not turned and galloped away? Would they have discovered then that they were irrevocably in love? And if they had, what a difference it might have made.

She heard the front door slam and her father's heavy step in the hall. "Still up, my dear?" he said, entering the library and crossing to the hearth to warm his hands in front of the fire. "It's bitterly cold outside."

"I know—I went skating this afternoon in Central Park."

"With Freddie?"

"No, I was alone."

"Come to think of it," he remarked, "I rarely see you alone. In fact I rarely see you at all except at the breakfast table. So this is quite an event finding you here. Would you care for a glass of sherry to celebrate?"

"Yes, that would be nice," she answered him lethargically.

He poured her sherry and brandy for himself. As he handed her the crystal glass he gave her a worried look. "You know," he said, "I often suspect you believe I'm so occupied with the sporting pages of the newspaper or going to my clubs that I give little thought to anything else, but on the contrary I'm much more observant than you think."

"What have you been observing?" she asked, struggling to speak lightly.

"I've been observing that you don't appear very happy for a girl who is betrothed and will be married in a few months. What's the matter?"

He sat down on the sofa beside her and gently tipped back her head, forcing her to face him directly. Angrily she brushed tears from her cheeks.

"For one thing, I'm certain you don't love Freddie," he continued. "Nevertheless, as you act very much to me like a girl head over heels in love, I can only come to one conclusion—there's someone else. Who is it?"

She paused on the brink of confessing and, deciding against it, took a sip of sherry before saying, "There's no one else, but you're right, of course. I don't love Freddie, although I've grown to care for him very much."

"You've grown to care for him very much," her father repeated. "That's not enough. In addition, I'm afraid I can't believe you when you say there's no one else. Who is it, Abigail? You might as well tell me, for if you don't, somehow I'll find out."

Staring into the fire, she whispered with trembling lips, "It's Archibald Pomeroy."

Chauncey Worth let out a low whistle. "Archibald Pomeroy! I never suspected you had more than a nodding acquaintanceship with him."

"No one knew except Hortense. I confided in her one day. He was at Saratoga for the entire month of August. We met there frequently."

"If that's the case, why in the world didn't he decide to ask then and there for your hand?"

"It was not as simple as that. He was already betrothed to Lady Ursula and had this fixed notion that I was far too frivolous and immature for him. I became angry and—"

Chauncey Worth broke in. "Let me guess. You became angry and retaliated by announcing your betrothal to Freddie. I always believed that happened too suddenly. I suppose at the time that seemed to settle the matter, until the Pomeroys returned to New York and, seeing Archibald again, you knew you were still in love with him."

"Yes," Abigail replied. "That's exactly what happened."

"Does Archibald now return your love?"

"Oh, yes," Abigail cried out breathlessly. "He told me so today in Central Park. It wasn't a planned meeting, Father. I hadn't the slightest suspicion he would be there. I fell and hit my head on the ice. When I opened my eyes there he was, bending over me—so tender, so loving. After that it was impossible for us to pretend any longer, to attempt to deny our feelings."

Her father shook his head slowly, frowning deeply. "So you told him you loved him. He said he loved you, and you parted with great sorrow, two star-crossed lovers caught in a trap, each betrothed to another, too foolishly loyal to break their promises."

"How did you guess?" she exclaimed in amazement.

"I guessed because your mother and I went down the very same road many years ago. We were both betrothed and not to each other when we fell in love."

"You never told me!"

"It happened so long ago." There was a sweet

reminiscent smile on his lips. "It never crossed my mind to tell you. As you are well aware, it has always been most difficult for me to discuss your mother. You see, I loved her very deeply. Besides, I had almost forgotten our elopement—the pain we went through, the anguish we suffered, until we gathered up enough courage to take a stand, until we finally admitted we could not exist apart."

"You eloped!" Abigail exclaimed. "I can't believe it."

"We certainly did, but I don't blame you for being surprised. It's difficult, I imagine, for the very young to visualize that a man on the far side of middle age was once impetuous and passionate and terribly, terribly in love."

"You said that you gathered up enough courage?"

"Exactly—it took courage, for it caused a bit of a scandal. To us the step seemed a horrendous one to take, but it was amazing how soon the uproar died down and our elopement was forgotten. In the long run your mother and I never doubted that what we did was without question the fairest step to take."

"You said you were betrothed to another woman?"

"Yes, she was very pleasant and attractive and I thought I loved her until your mother entered my life."

"The other girl—what happened to her?"

"She survived very nicely. In fact it wasn't too long before I suspect she was grateful for my honesty. She married less than a year later. I've been told it has been a highly successful relationship."

"Are you advising me to elope with Archibald Pomeroy?"

"No, I'm not advising, I'm telling you." He took her limp hand in his and squeezed it tightly. "If you don't, there will be nothing but regrets for the rest of your life, Abigail. Surely you don't believe that you can make Freddie happy feeling as you do? He'll only end up being miserable too."

He rose, refilling her glass with sherry. "Now, here's what you must do. Tomorrow you must get in touch with Archibald Pomeroy. I know young girls are not supposed to take the initiative in affairs of the heart, but in this situation, I consider that nonsense. Therefore, you must see him and tell him what I have told you tonight."

She shook her head doubtfully. "He's extremely stubborn."

Her father's eyes were twinkling. "I was stubborn too."

"What about Clarissa?" An expression of despair crossed Abigail's face.

"Forget Clarissa. Of course, she will be properly horrified. But don't worry, I can handle that." He chuckled. "Poor dear, she'll have to tear up a tremendous number of sheets of paper."

For the first time Abigail laughed. "All those plans for the wedding!"

"Yes, out the window they must go, but one step at a time, Abigail. There's no point in arousing Clarissa's ire until it's too late for her to do anything but sputter. I am forecasting a rapid recovery by your stepmother when she learns who you have decided to marry. Clarissa will find it difficult not to be pleased that you are marrying an ambassador's son."

He yawned and stretched wearily. "I'm getting far too old for emotional scenes. You must be exhausted too, my dear daughter." Bending down, he kissed her lightly on the forehead. "Go to bed," he admonished. "Sleep well, for I want you to be your most beautiful tomorrow when you meet with Archibald. Now don't worry. You'll see that everything will turn out as I have predicted."

Chapter Twenty-six

To her great surprise Abigail did sleep well, extremely well, and in the morning seated at the breakfast table, watching her father immersed in the sporting pages, she was beginning to wonder if what had occurred last night between them had been a dream. Until he looked up, gave her a conspiratorial wink, and said to his wife, "Clarissa, my pet, I've been worried for some time that you'll strain those lovely eyes of yours poring over your endless lists. It's a glorious winter's day. I've ordered a carriage and you and I are going for a ride and later out to lunch."

Clarissa, her face aglow at such an unusual but pleasant prospect, hurried from the breakfast room to dress.

"And you, Abigail," her father said breezily, "with the decks cleared, so to speak, have only one direction to go—full speed ahead."

Despite her father's advice, she lingered over her coffee, at first telling herself that it was far too early to take any action, devising all sorts of excuses to postpone the inevitable moment when she would be forced to take positive steps.

Pacing back and forth in her bedroom, she finally sat down at her desk and wrote a brief note to Archibald, slipping it into a white envelope and sealing it with wax. In it she briefly stated that it was imperative for them to meet.

She next surveyed her wardrobe, selecting a dark-blue-velvet suit to wear. She considered it the most becoming outfit in her extensive collection. It was perfectly tailored with a narrow ermine collar and an ermine hat to match.

Taking the note downstairs with her, she ordered a carriage, specifically requesting Tommy to drive, and she left for the Pomeroys' house with the message for Archibald hidden in her purse.

Several times on the short ride it was on the tip of her tongue to call out to Tommy to turn back. Last night in the library when her father had explained to her what she must do, it had seemed logical and plausible, and she had gone to bed assured that on the morrow, all would be well as her father had promised.

But now as the moment of confrontation drew near, she was seized with panic and grave foreboding. What if Archibald refused to meet with her? What if he did meet with her but remained adamant in his conviction that he had no recourse but to marry Lady Ursula?

The carriage halted in the driveway outside the massive oak doors of the Pomeroy mansion. Tommy hopped down from his seat to assist her. With burning cheeks and an unsteady hand, she drew her note to Archibald from her purse, proffering it to him.

"If young Mr. Pomeroy is about, please give the letter directly to him," she said in a shaky voice. "I'll wait in the carriage for his answer. If he isn't there, find out, if you can, where he can be reached."

In her anxiety it seemed to her that Tommy was gone for a very long time, but actually it was only a matter of minutes before he came bounding down the stone steps and scrambled back up onto the driver's seat.

"I left your message with the footman," he told her. "Mr. Pomeroy is out at the moment. He's gone to the Metropolitan Museum. Where to now, Miss Abigail?" He tossed her a curious glance.

"To the Metropolitan!" Abigail frowned, puzzled as to why he would be visiting the museum at this early hour, thoroughly deflated to have missed him.

As they drove along Fifth Avenue she began to wonder what she would do or say if she found Archibald not alone but with his fiancée and then realized it would be simple to explain she was there to view the Sargent collection. It had opened directly after Christmas, and she had been far too busy with parties and balls to attend.

When they reached the museum, instinct told her to go to the area where the Sargent portraits were on display. It was already crowded with patrons of art, and despite her anxiety as she entered, Abigail caught her breath, overcome by the splendor of his work.

Passing by his controversial painting of Madame X, considered his most daring work because the gown she was wearing was very décolleté, she saw her mother's portrait on the opposite wall and moving toward it found Archibald Pomeroy, seated on a cushioned bench, his eyes fastened on the priceless painting of the first Mrs. Chauncey Worth.

He did not notice her approach—all of his attention was riveted on the portrait. Joining him on the bench, she said softly, "She's very lovely, isn't she?"

He started at the sound of her voice, and when he turned to her and saw her sitting beside him, he drew in his breath sharply. "Yes," he replied, "and you are so much like her. I promised yesterday never to see you again, Abigail, so this seemed the next-best way to say good-bye."

"Must we say farewell?" she asked, her voice just above a whisper. "Is there no other solution?"

"No—not an honorable one."

"My father does not agree. We had a wonderful

talk last night. I confessed to him that I loved you and you loved me, and do you know what he said?"

When Archibald did not reply she continued. "He told me that people truly in love should marry. That it was the only answer. And then he revealed to me something I had never suspected. He said he and my mother eloped. Did you realize that?"

"No, I didn't."

"Your mother must have been aware of it and has never said a word. There must be many people, too, who have long since forgotten all about it, so I guess it didn't really make too much of a stir."

"What are you trying to say?"

"I'm saying it's wrong to deny love—real love. My father explained all that to me last night. My parents were betrothed too, but not to each other when they met. Isn't that a strange coincidence?"

"And no one remembers it now?" he asked.

"No, it was a scandal quickly forgotten. He advises us to follow in their footsteps. He told me I could never make Freddie happy loving you the way I do, and how do you suppose you could make Ursula content? Anyway, no matter what happens between you and me, I've decided I can't marry Freddie."

His eyes were shining. "Funny, but I've reached the same conclusion. I made up my mind last night that it would be impossible for me to marry Ursula, and I've been gathering up my courage to tell her so."

"I love you, Archibald," she said simply.

"And I love you, Abigail," he replied.

Oblivious to the large number of people surrounding them, he gathered her in his arms and kissed her the way he had been longing to do since their meeting that August morning at Kayaderosseras Creek, when they had embraced for the first time and she had galloped off on Matilda.

They wandered through the long galleries of the Metropolitan, hand in hand, forming plans, discarding them, knowing now that it would all work out in the end, that nothing could ever separate them again. While gazing at her mother's portrait they had taken the first step toward a wonderful life together.

"I don't enjoy living in the city," he told her.

"Neither do I."

"Perhaps we could buy a farm somewhere in New England. You wouldn't be bored there while I wrote?"

"Of course not. I could never be bored with you." She was smiling up at him.

"Smile like that again," he begged. "You're adorable when you smile." In the next breath he was asking how and when they could be married.

"We're not making much sense," she complained as they darted from one subject to another.

"Who wants to make sense!" he exclaimed, and they were in each other's arms again.

It was Abigail who belatedly remembered that poor Tommy had been waiting for sometime outside with her carriage, and they hurried from the museum to find him.

"I'll tell Freddie tonight," she promised.

"And I'll tell Ursula."

As they journeyed homeward he pulled her close to him once more, kissing the tip of her nose. "My mother will be extremely happy," he murmured.

Abigail laughed. "My stepmother will be extremely difficult, but father has assured me he can handle that situation, and I think she'll soon come round."

Reaching her father's town house, they did not stir from the carriage until Tommy, who was waiting patiently for them to remember where they were, tipped his cap and said with grave formality, "I believe congratulations are in order, Miss Abigail."

"Yes—thank you, Tommy," she cried out joyfully and, smiling up at Archibald Pomeroy, she said with a mischievous grin, "You see, our secret is out, so we can't back down now, Archibald. As my father said this morning at breakfast—there's only one way for you to go, Abigail—full steam ahead."

But they still did not make a move to leave the carriage, remaining close to each other, hands clasped, in a world of their own until Tommy, clearing his throat nervously, said with a slight stammer, "Excuse me—Miss Abigail—but will you be needing the carriage?"

"Poor Tommy!" Abigail cried out, reluctantly returning to reality. "Your lips are blue with the cold. No, I don't need the carriage. Please return it to the stables at once and then seek out cook in the kitchen for some hot soup."

With Tommy's help she descended gracefully to the ground and, glancing up at Archibald with a tremulous smile, invited him to accompany her into the house.

"Your father," she said, "is not the only skilled diplomat I know, for I have discovered that my father has much the same attributes. Only this morning he asked my stepmother out for a drive and luncheon, which gives us a little time to catch our breaths and decide what we should do."

Alone in the library, in front of a roaring fire, they made a valiant but fairly fruitless attempt to become sober and sensible as they planned their future together.

"I'll tell Freddie tonight," Abigail promised again.

"And I'll tell Ursula," Archibald replied again

before gathering her in his arms. As they kissed he wondered how he had ever been so short sighted as to have believed for one instant that Lady Ursula Huntington could have brought him such happiness.

"I don't want to elope," Abigail confessed much later, pulling away from him so she could trace with her fingers the outline of his strong, regular features. "Not that I want an elaborate formal wedding," she hastened to add. "That's not what I want. But if we run off somewhere, it would appear as if we were ashamed of what we were doing, and I'm not ashamed at all, are you?"

"Ashamed? Of course not! On the contrary, I'm proud, terribly proud. We'll be married wherever you say—in Central Park or by the Kayaderosseras Creek if that's what you desire, but I make only one proviso, it must be soon."

They kissed once more, a long, lingering kiss, oblivious to the fact that they were no longer alone in the library, startled when Clarissa Worth's cold, clear voice punctured the aura of bliss surrounding them.

"I am horrified," she exclaimed. "Completely horrified!"

Swinging about, they saw her standing in the doorway, an imposing figure, still wearing her mink hat and cloak, her cheeks aflame with indignation.

Chauncey Worth stood beside her. "My dear

Clarissa," he interposed, "I meant to bring the subject up at luncheon, but we were having such a delightful tête-à-tête, it slipped my mind."

"You knew about this?" Clarissa stormed, turning upon him like an avenging angel. "You knew about this and never said one word to me. I warned you, Chauncey Worth, this summer in Saratoga that Abigail was headed for disaster, and now you are telling me that you condone your daughter's actions—betrothed to one man and dallying with another, who I've been led to believe is also betrothed."

"Clarissa," Abigail exclaimed, instinctively rushing to her father's defense. "Father didn't know until last night that I was in love with Archibald. Also, I'm not a strumpet, if that's what you are implying. I plan to see Freddie tonight to end our engagement, while Archibald will meet with Ursula with the same purpose in mind." Her eyes were flashing in anger, her hands clenched to do battle, until she saw her father shake his head in warning, giving her a surreptitious wink.

"Well," Chauncey Worth said heartily, "as it seems to be settled, I believe congratulations are in order."

"Your congratulations!" Clarissa snapped. Crossing to a sofa by the hearth, she sank into it with a moan of despair. "The scandal," she cried out, "the scandal. And what about the wedding invitations, the bridesmaids' dresses, and my gown? Why, I even ordered the wedding cake last week, hired the musicians for the reception, and Reverend Hutchinson has agreed to officiate. How will we ever live this down?"

"Quite easily, my dear Clarissa," Chauncey Worth replied, pouring himself a liberal glass of port. "Will you join me, Archibald," he asked, "in a toast welcoming you most warmly into our family?" He savored the port with pleasure. "And you, Clarissa, my pet," he continued, "could do with a spot of sherry—Abigail as well." But Clarissa merely tossed him a withering look and with great dignity stalked out of the room.

"Time will heal her wounds," Chauncey Worth remarked with an understanding smile. "And now, my children, what are your plans?"

"Archibald and I were just saying, Father, that we really don't want to elope."

"I agree," her father replied, raising his glass of port to his future son-in-law. "It's far too late for that, for I believe if you look up the word 'elope' in the dictionary, you will discover it is defined as running away secretly without parental consent. Therefore, as your intentions are no longer a secret and I gladly give you my blessing, elopement seems to be quite out of the question. Perhaps a quiet ceremony here at home would prove to be a happy compromise." He kissed his only daughter fondly on both cheeks.

* * *

Of course, they found it difficult to break their betrothals, but they did so that very evening, as they had promised. Afterward they decided on a simple wedding ceremony the following Saturday.

Only Clarissa Worth remained adamant, refusing to take any part in the preparations or to attend the wedding, until Edwina Pomeroy, delighted by the unexpected turn of events, invited her to tea.

"I understand," she said sympathetically to Clarissa as she plied her with wafer-thin sandwiches and tiny frosted cakes, "how difficult this whole affair has been for you—for all of us, as a matter of fact, for no one wants to unwittingly hurt another human being. But surely you have noticed how very much in love Abigail and Archibald are. Therefore I'm certain, my dear, that you will soon find it in your heart to forgive them."

When Clarissa did not reply, Mrs. Pomeroy touched on other topics—discussing how wonderful England was in the springtime and how she was hoping now they were about to be connected by marriage that the Chauncey Worths would honor them with a visit to the Embassy.

"I can't promise you'll meet the queen," she said smoothly, "for, as you are well aware, she has long since become a recluse. But without question while you are with us, we will entertain the Prince and Princess of Wales, and I would be very much surprised if we did not receive an invitation to Sandringham or Marlborough House. You'll find them delightful company."

As she spoke Clarissa Worth felt her defenses crumbling, entranced as she was by the prospect of being entertained for the London Season. In the end, the tea party turned out to be a great success, concluding with she and Mrs. Pomeroy reaching a first-name basis and discussing what gowns they would wear to Abigail and Archibald's wedding.

The wedding that Saturday was a beautiful ceremony, with their parents present and Hortense and Harold Staunton as their only attendants. It took place in the drawing room of the Worths' town house, with the first Mrs. Worth's portrait over the mantel, reminding them that she had played a vital role in the happy ending to their romance.

They spent their honeymoon at The Elms, discovering that Saratoga in the winter becomes a sleepy village, hidden in the snow, the ideal spot for a newly married couple to begin their life together.

In the spring they traveled to England in time to see Archibald's first novel published, lingering on for the London Season, attending the balls, races, and weekend house parties in the country.

Clarissa and Chauncey Worth joined them there and Clarissa, to her delight, was introduced to the very apex of London society, storing up a goodly supply of amusing anecdotes to relay to her friends and acquaintances in New York and Saratoga.

Chauncey Worth attended the races at Ascot and discovered that gambling at Boodle's and White's was much the same as in his own clubs in New York or at Canfield's Casino.

The news of their marriage jolted the little world they occupied, and after the wedding their names were on everybody's lips for a week or maybe two until as Chauncey Worth had predicted, a much more shocking scandal came along to take its place.

In less than a year Freddie Freyhuysing, fully recuperated, married Sally Whitney and everyone agreed it turned out to be a most successful marriage.

Lady Ursula Huntington returned to England, where she rode to the hounds and joined the suffragettes, telling everyone she considered marriage an outdated custom as well as a terrific bore.

It was not very long until the names of Abigail and Archibald Pomeroy caused scarcely a ripple among the upper classes in Saratoga, New York, and London, for what is there to discuss about two young people who fall in love, marry, and are content to spend the rest of their lives together?

They were considered to be a very happy couple. "A perfect match," Clarissa Worth was fond of saying, and Abigail Pomeroy, whenever she heard her stepmother make that comment, smiled and was thankful that at last she and her stepmother had reached an agreement on a very important subject.

Love—the way you want it!

Candlelight Romances

	TITLE NO.	
☐ **A MAN OF HER CHOOSING** by Nina Pykare $1.50	#554	(15133-3)
☐ **PASSING FANCY** by Mary Linn Roby $1.50	#555	(16770-1)
☐ **THE DEMON COUNT** by Anne Stuart $1.25	#557	(11906-5)
☐ **WHERE SHADOWS LINGER** by Janis Susan May ...$1.25	#556	(19777-5)
☐ **OMEN FOR LOVE** by Esther Boyd $1.25	#552	(16108-8)
☐ **MAYBE TOMORROW** by Marie Pershing $1.25	#553	(14909-6)
☐ **LOVE IN DISGUISE** by Nina Pykare $1.50	#548	(15229-1)
☐ **THE RUNAWAY HEIRESS** by Lillian Cheatham $1.50	#549	(18083-X)
☐ **HOME TO THE HIGHLANDS** by Jessica Eliot $1.25	#550	(13104-9)
☐ **DARK LEGACY** by Candace Connell $1.25	#551	(11771-2)
☐ **LEGACY OF THE HEART** by Lorena McCourtney ...$1.25	#546	(15645-9)
☐ **THE SLEEPING HEIRESS** by Phyllis Taylor Pianka ...$1.50	#543	(17551-8)
☐ **DAISY** by Jennie Tremaine $1.50	#542	(11683-X)
☐ **RING THE BELL SOFTLY** by Margaret James $1.25	#545	(17626-3)
☐ **GUARDIAN OF INNOCENCE** by Judy Boynton $1.25	#544	(11862-X)
☐ **THE LONG ENCHANTMENT** by Helen Nuelle $1.25	#540	(15407-3)
☐ **SECRET LONGINGS** by Nancy Kennedy $1.25	#541	(17609-3)

At your local bookstore or use this handy coupon for ordering:

Dell **DELL BOOKS**
P.O. BOX 1000, PINEBROOK, N.J. 07058

Please send me the books I have checked above. I am enclosing $ _____
(please add 75¢ per copy to cover postage and handling). Send check or money order—no cash or C.O.D.'s. Please allow up to 8 weeks for shipment.

Mr/Mrs/Miss _____

Address _____

City _____ State/Zip _____

INTRODUCING...

Romantique

The Romance Magazine For The 1980's

Each exciting issue contains a full-length romance novel — the kind of first-love story we all dream about...

PLUS

other wonderful features such as a travelogue to the world's most romantic spots, advice about your romantic problems, a quiz to find the ideal mate for you and much, much more.

ROMANTIQUE: A complete novel of romance, plus a whole world of romantic features.

ROMANTIQUE: Wherever magazines are sold. Or write Romantique Magazine, Dept. C-1, 41 East 42nd Street, New York, N.Y. 10017

Romantique

INTERNATIONALLY DISTRIBUTED BY DELL DISTRIBUTING, INC.